The Salt Slave

GRACE TRIUMPHS

George Thomas Smith

authorHOUSE®

AuthorHouse™
1663 Liberty Drive
Bloomington, IN 47403
www.authorhouse.com
Phone: 1-800-839-8640

First published by AuthorHouse 11/17/2011

ISBN: 978-1-4678-7025-2 (e)
ISBN: 978-1-4678-7026-9 (sc)

Library of Congress Control Number: 2011960486

Printed in the United States of America

The Prelude

This story, "The Salt Slave," is a snap shot of history during the days of the Roman Empire. It is of one fictional family's tragedies and struggles for ultimate meaning in a world where injustice for certain groups of people prevailed.

"The Salt Slave" creates the account of a grandfather, Abdi, a father, Andrew, and his son, Eliab, who in the first century were overwhelmed by the events that impacted the relationship between the Jews and the Romans. Rome sought absolute domination of two particular groups of people: Jews and Christians. These two groups struggled for survival and freedom against gigantic odds. In the unfolding of those days a Jewish family became conflicted over the events that included the Roman execution of a man many believed to be the Jewish Messiah, the sack and destruction of Jerusalem, the horrific events surrounding the Roman assault of Masada, and the life of a boy who wrestled with why he was so often spared when others succumbed to deadly Roman persecution. He found his answer after years of resisting the ultimate truth.

The Roman destruction of Jerusalem under General Titus was the seventeenth such event in the history of that city, dating from the time it was taken by the men of Judah. Throughout its entire history Jerusalem was destroyed in one degree of another twenty-seven times and, according to the Book of the Revelation, it will again be invaded and sacked by a future world dictator.

During the account of the family's struggles, Eliab Marcus grows from a child to an adult. He is pulled in different directions by the events of those days including the conflicting influences of his family, the political chaos, and his own wrestling with where he fits as a Jewish boy in a Roman world that is being challenged by a new and dynamic faith centered in a man who, though killed by Romans, became more powerful in the lives of first century humanity than he was before his death.

Contents

CHAPTER ONE

Escape to Masada

The Roman General Titus and his vast legions of battle hardened soldiers had one thing in mind: destroy Jerusalem and everyone in it. Many people fled east across the Jordan River. Others, out of sheer desperation, scattered southward into the barren Negeve. A band of Zealots led by a man named Eleazar descended the four thousand feet from upper Judea and Jerusalem to the foreboding region of the Dead Sea. The nearly one thousand escapees included women and children. They resorted to the rugged, parched, waterless wilderness for safety.

In the writings of the ancient Jewish historian, Josephus, it has been learned that Masada was first fortified by someone he called, "Johnatan the High Priest." It is not known if this person was actually Judah "the Hammer" of the Maccabeans, or another man whose name was Alexander. History is somewhat clouded in this matter. Whoever the person was, he no doubt recognized Masada as a natural fortification rising several hundred feet above the sand that surrounded it. It was there in that remote location that the Zealots made their stand.

From his position in one of the towers on Masada, a Zealot named Naphish looked north and west over the vast, parched wilderness of southern Judea. For a long time he gazed at nothing but shimmering heat, dust devils, and the clear blue sky as far as he could see. To the north were the rugged, rocky outcroppings where the terrain began to rise toward the mountainous spine of his homeland.

Shading his eyes from the blazing sun, the heavily bearded man peered more intently. Was it the heat rising from the desert, or did he actually see something? There it was, or was it? Yes! There really was something moving far to the north. It appeared to be a barely noticeable swirling cloud rising from the desert.

Naphish ran across the compound to find the leader of the Zealots, shouting his name all the way. "Eleazar! Eleazar! Come quickly! From the northwest tower I have seen something!"

"And what would that something be, my excitable friend?"

"A cloud of dust! The Romans are coming!"

Eleazar climbed the steps of the tower and peered into the distance. He was calm. He was not a man to show any sign of anxiety. Many of his followers believed he feared nothing or no one. His appearance as that of an authority figure was enhanced by steely brown eyes and a graying beard. "So, those heathen dogs have decided to make a fight of it after all. It had to be. We couldn't stay on this rock forever nor will the Romans let us. Alert the compound that we will have company soon."

"How soon, Eleazar?

"They will have to stop and rest before they get here. I imagine they will be within two hours of Masada by early evening. Perhaps they will make a permanent camp while their commanders decide on just how to try to reach the top of this place. Many will wish they had never come south."

While Naphish hastily spread the word of the approaching Roman legions, the tyrannical Eleazer, who had ensconced himself and his followers on the top of the huge rock formation rising up from the wilderness, watched as the columns of soldiers grew closer until individuals could finally be seen.

Soon, it became evident that the dust being raised was not all the result of the Roman legions. There were several thousands of other people trailing the Roman columns and guarded by other soldiers. "Slaves!" Eleazar snarled. "Jewish slaves!"

Naphish had just returned to the tower and heard his leader's exclamation. "Eleazar, why would they have a need of slaves?"

"I'm not sure, Naphish, but we will know in a day or two."

*

It had been nearly two years since General Titus marched on Jerusalem, sacked the city, murdered the inhabitants, and tore down the Temple. The Romans had put up with the rebellious Jews long enough. It wasn't satisfying for Rome to see a million Jews dead and many more scattered into the deserts, so Governor Flavius Silva determined it was time to destroy the hold-outs encamped on Masada.

Masada was an unusual rock formation that rose up from the desert west of the Dead Sea. Its flat top had a rhomboid shape which was longer than it was wide with only a few very difficult trails snaking up the vertical face of the rock. The formation reached more than eight hundred feet on the east side and six hundred feet on the west.

Herod the Great, who was king during the time of Jesus' birth, added to the height of the promontory by building a twenty foot wall around the entire perimeter thirty-five years before Jesus of Nazareth was born. After Jerusalem fell to the Parthians, a few years prior to Herod's building of fortifications, the Edumean king fled to Masada with members of his family for protection from the danger he faced from the Jews he ruled as well as the invaders.

Herod provided storehouses for grain, dates, other staples, and, of course, wine. There was a thin layer of sandy soil on the top of the mighty rock, but it was enough to grow vegetables and grain which was cultivated and watered by hand. The scarcity of useable water required it to be brought from a distance and stored. Besides housing the necessities to sustain life for an extended period of time, Masada's fortress had an accumulation of weapons, as well as ingots of iron and other metals from which there could be forged more weapons for an army as large as ten thousand men. Now, it was a band of Zealots occupying Herod's retreat. The Zealots were the last group to provide any organized form of resistance to the Romans.

As people watched from the guard towers that had been incorporated into Herod's wall, the approaching columns of the Tenth Legion and its auxiliary troops divided. One column split in a southerly direction and encamped on the west side of Masada and the other marched eastward along the north side of the rock. The mass of slaves halted their approach until Flavius Silva would find a use for them. He surely knew what labor he had in mind for those who were expendable.

Naphish sounded worried as well as curious. "Eleazar, what are they doing?"

"It is called encirclement. It looks like the larger force is moving to the north approach. The others will protect against any attempts to escape. Escape is not an option for us. Set guards at the top of all the trails. The Romans may send scouts to see if we are on alert."

It was Flavius' intention to end all Jewish resistance at the rock and he was prepared for a long siege. As the Zealots watched from Masada, the Romans established eight camps on the desert floor. Over the next several weeks they proceeded to build a wall around the base of Masada to assure that those on the top of the rock could not escape Rome's wrath.

Eleazar called the primary leaders of his community together to make preparation for the coming assault. "Have the people gather every stone they can find and break larger rock into useful projectiles. Put the majority of the stones on the north wall. That looks like the side they intend to use to reach us."

Weeks dragged on into months while the ten to fifteen thousand Jewish prisoners Flavius brought with him labored in the sand, sun, and scorpions to build an earthen ramp up the north wall of Masada. It took nine months, but finally the ramp, consisting of earth with tons of rocks, provided the foundation for the siege tower. The foundation was 100 feet wide and firm enough that the assault tower was ready to be constructed. The tower was framed in wood and clad in iron. The height was nearly 120 feet. It was an amazing accomplishment for the location and conditions. While that was being done, the defenders did their best to harass the workers who moved up and down the earthen ramp and framework of the tower like ants.

The Zealots did what they could to slow down the process, but they knew they would not stop the construction of the tower and the catapults erected upon it. Those who knew how to use slings did some damage, but it was only a defensive effort. The inevitability of the Roman breakthrough weighed on everyone's mind, especially the women and children.

Among the older children was Eliab Marcus who did his best to distract the younger ones by organizing games and leading in the singing of folk songs. If he had his choice, he would be a warrior. Eliab had developed a great hatred for the Romans because of his parents' deaths at the hands of the Jerusalem invaders.

After nine months, the day dawned when fiery arrows and other missiles were launched from catapults. These projectiles rained down upon the Zealots and the structures they used for protection. This went on for days and then weeks until a battering ram was employed successfully. It bashed through the perimeter stone wall on the north side, but the defenders had built an inner wall of earth and wood that was flexible and more difficult to break than King Herod's stone wall. However, the wood also began to fracture. The Romans resorted to fire as a means of burning through the inner wall.

Assault efforts ceased at night and that gave Eleazar time to gather his people to begin to execute their own plan. First, they set fire to all their possessions. There would be nothing left for the Roman soldiers to gather as spoils of war. Next, ten men were chosen and charged with performing what Eleazar considered mercy killings. The Zealots would not allow themselves to be executed at the hands of the Romans, nor would they submit to lives of slavery.

The chosen ten were to make sure that each father had killed his wife and children and then himself. After that, the ten did the same with their own families and committed suicide. It was decided that one person would be spared. The intention was to send that person down the side of Masada facing the Dead Sea by way of whatever length of rope the Zealots could fashion. This lone individual would then have to make his way on to the ground the best he could.

There was a good chance that whoever was elected to be the one lowered from the top of the rock would fall once he no longer had the rope to which he could cling. He would have to feel his way in the darkness. Hand holds and places to set his feet would be difficult to find.

The next problem, should he manage by a miracle to reach the desert sand, was to make his way through the Roman encirclement.

Eliab Marcus was chosen to try to escape and tell others all that happened on Masada; especially how the people bravely died in an act of defiance. Eliab had gladly joined in the dream of freeing Israel from the heathen hoards of the Roman Empire. He expected to be martyred, but instead he was to be a messenger so that others could know what took place that night before the Romans' final assault.

On the last morning of the battle for Masada, the Romans began to stream through the breach in the inner wall. They met no resistance. The loud battle cries of the soldiers as they entered the compound soon died away to a sudden and strange silence. The legions surrounding the base of Masada heard the initial charge and then all went quiet. Was the battle over that quickly?

The attacking force on top of the monolith began to search through the ashes and remaining structures. Masada was deathly quiet, except for the sounds of the Roman soldiers' heavy battle sandals and the clanking of their protective metal. The place had become a tomb and a monument to Jewish resistance and the 960 souls who died there.

The Romans had their victory, but it was empty. The only life the soldiers found on the rock was that of two women and five children who had hidden in a cave and were missed in the mass murder-suicide. The Romans did not find the various scrolls of the sacred scriptures that were hidden and preserved from desecration by the pagan hordes.

At the moment the legions poured onto Masada with the loud roar of battle cries, the auxiliary units waited to see if there would be any Jews trying to escape, but they soon heard the trumpet sounding the signal to withdraw. With that, those troops at the base of the rock began to move back to their encampments. News spread quickly that the Zealots were dead. It was believed there was no further need to protect against an escape once the body of Eleazar was found among the others.

Tucked into a cleft in the east face of the gigantic rock formation, and about half way down, was a lone, frightened boy. Eliab waited quietly all day until the light began to fade and the side of Masada where he was hiding fell into the shadow of the rock. Slowly he moved out of his concealment and painstakingly, with extreme care, descended from foothold to foothold until he at last found the ground beneath his feet. By then, it was too dark to go anywhere safely. He would have to wait until the sun began to rise again. It would be a cold night.

Very early the next morning Eliab Marcus moved away from the base of Masada down some fifty more feet to the shore of the Dead Sea. He took advantage of the dim light to put distance between him and the Roman encampments. The night air had chilled him, but with the rising of the sun it would not be long until the glowing sphere would break above the mountains on the east side of the Sea. When that happened, the heat would become a problem.

What little drinking water Eliab had would not last long and there was none to be found from the salty Dead Sea. He needed to make his way north to where the Jordan River emptied. There he could rest. There he could find water to go with the pieces of bread that he had stuffed inside his garment. Besides hunger and thirst, there was the matter of loneliness. His destination was to find some Jews who had escaped from Jerusalem across the Jordan River to the east. He would tell them about Masada and he would lend his good right arm to taking a life for a life from the Roman murderers.

Nine miles north of Masada, along the coast of the Dead See, Eliab came across a stream that emptied into the salty water. It was nearly dry, but contained enough liquid to quench his thirst temporarily. He had only a small bladder of a lamb in which he was able to carry water with him. Additionally, Eliab saturated his neck scarf in the stream and wrapped it around his head for some relief from the sun. He would not drink any more water until the next day. After that, the boy knew he could only take a few small swallows each day until he reached the upper end of the Dead Sea. At a point south of Bethabara, he hoped to cross the Jordan and make his way due east toward Esbus where he prayed he might find other dispersed Zealots.

Walking over very rough ground in the blistering heat of the wasteland required frequent rest stops which also added time to Eliab's effort to reach his goal. The nights were bitter cold for the clothes he was wearing and the days were as hot as the nights were cold. It took three days to go from Masada to the crossing of the Jordan. It was three days of practically nothing to eat. At the end of that time, Eliab stumbled into Esbus and fainted before he could draw water from the well. When he awakened, it was dark and he found himself in the tent of a shepherd.

"Where am I?"

"You know, boy, I could have prophesied that would be the first thing you would say when you finally finished sleeping."

"I am no boy! I am thirteen and that makes me a man!"

"It makes you old enough to be a man, but it doesn't make you a man just because you are old enough."

"I am too tired to argue with you. Why did you bring me here and what is your name?"

The elderly man with a face leathered and darkened by living in the sun laughed. "My, you have a lot of questions. Well, I brought you here because it was not safe to leave you in the dust beside the well. Another shepherd's sheep might have walked all over your scrawny looking body. Besides that, you were in the way of my sheep. As for my name, it is Lehabin. What is your name?"

"It is Eliab."

"And why did I find you passed out on the ground?"

"I have come a long way and have not eaten for days."

Lehabin motioned to a woman standing at the flap of the tent to bring some meat from the fire several feet away. "My wife will give you some roasted lamb and milk and then I want to know more about this orphan I have found."

Eliab ate like the starved boy he was and when he was full the questions began again. "Son, where is your family?"

"Before I answer your question, please tell me are you a son of Abraham?"

"And if I say that I am not, what then?"

"Then I will tell you nothing!"

"You are certainly a stubborn boy."

"I told you I am a man! It takes a man to survive what I have been through. So, are you a son of Abraham?"

"Yes, Eliab, I have made sacrifices at the temple in Jerusalem, when there still was a temple."

"But are you a Zealot?"

"I am too old to be a Zealot, but I believe in the cause."

Eliab sat up straight. "Then I will tell you about Masada."

That comment got the shepherd's attention. "What about Masada?"

"That is where I just came from! The Zealots encamped there are all dead! I was helped to escape to tell others about what happened."

Lehabin took the boy by his shoulders and looked him in the eyes. "When did you become part of the community on Masada and how did they all die?"

Chapter Two
Another Hill

The shepherd, Lehabin, who found Eliab and provided him with food and shelter, was anxious to hear what the survivor from Masada had to say, but he also wanted others to listen, so he sent his wife to gather two under-shepherds to join them in the tent.

"Now, Eliab, tell us about what happened at Masada."

"I will, but first I must tell you about my family, so be patient with me. It was because of what happened to my family that I was taken with the Zealots to the desert. It starts with my grandfather, Abdi, who was 58 years old at the time the Romans crucified the man named Jesus. Many thought he might be the long awaited Messiah, but grandfather, who was a devout member of the priesthood, refused to believe that Jesus was the promised One."

The shepherds leaned closer to hear the boy relate what he had learned from his family about the man named Jesus.

"My father told me years later what happened when it was time for my grandfather to take his turn to serve at the temple. He and my father, Andrew, were passing by the Praetorium when they saw a huge crowd of people. Father said the people were shouting and making a great deal of noise. He and grandfather Abdi could not see what was happening, but they waited on the edge of the crowd until all grew quiet, except for the sound of a whip as it crack in the air and found the object of a Roman soldier's anger. Again and again there was the crack of the whip and the thud of hitting flesh."

Eliab paused to take a sip of water before he continued to speak of what he had been told. He then described how Abdi and Andrew followed as the crowd became smaller. The onlookers moved as one mass toward the city wall and through the gate to a place some called Golgatha. It was a place where the Romans executed criminals. The two men watched as a man carrying a huge beam of wood staggered up the grade to the top of the hill. Even from the edge of the crowd they could see the bloody result of the Roman flogging. It was designed to weaken the condemned so that he would not be strong enough to prolong his time on the cross.

Abdi and his son watched as Jesus was placed on the crossbeam and spikes driven through his wrists. They heard the gasps and sobs of a group of women who stood nearby. In stunned silence, the two men observed the methodical process as soldiers hoisted the beam with the man attached to it until it was affixed to the vertical wooden stake. Then the two parts were combined. A spike was driven through the feet of the man on the center cross to secure them to the stake.

Many of the people who passed by the crosses cast insults and accusations at Jesus as they mocked him. Many had followed him because they thought he would perform miracles that would be a benefit to them and give them a more comfortable life, but now they were upset because they did not understand why he wasn't who they thought he was.

Abdi wanted to leave the hill, but Andrew could not take his eyes from the scene being played out before him. He urged his father to move closer so that they could hear what the man on the cross was saying, but Abdi refused. "If you want to stay here and see this gruesome event, that is your choice, but I have work in the Temple. The man is a false Messiah. He deserves what he is getting for deceiving so many fools." With that retort, Abdi made his way back down the hill and then back up to the city.

Andrew moved into and then through the gathered group of curiosity seekers. Some were there because they were followers of the victim, but others were there for the macabre entertainment. Andrew felt a strange compulsion to take in the event as though the only two persons on that hill were him and the man nailed to the Roman cross. Everyone and everything else faded from view. He didn't even hear the sobbing of the women. It was as though the words Jesus spoke from time to time over the next three hours were just for Andrew.

"What did he say?"

The man next to Andrew replied, "What did who say what?"

"The man on the middle cross just said something. What was it?"

Another man leaned over toward Andrew, "He said that his father should forgive those who were crucifying him."

"Did he mean father Abraham, or Jehovah?"

"Don't ask me. I just know what he said."

Immediately there was a darkening of the mid day sky as if it was midnight and then the earth shook. People clung to each other. Some could not stand and fell to the ground in fear.

Andrew groped his way to the front of the confused crowd of people, who for those dark hours had nothing to gawk at because of the blackness. A little later he heard the man from Nazareth speaking with one of the two men who were being crucified with him. It sounded like Jesus told the convicted thief that they would be together in Paradise. How could this be? The idea that such persons, who were being punished for crimes, would be rewarded with Paradise just didn't make sense to Andrew.

Time passed so slowly as the people waited to hear what would happen next. Some of them had been to several crucifixions and they were used to hearing cursing and railing against the authorities. Some even begged for death to end their suffering while others shouted their innocence until they had no strength left to protest.

The other man hanging on a nearby cross spoke to the Nazarene and bitterly complained and mocked Jesus for having claimed to be the Son of God, but who was now powerless to come down off the cross to save himself. That accusation caused Andrew to question in his own mind all the things he had heard about Jesus being the Messiah.

Later, Andrew heard Jesus say to one of the women that she should behold her son. At first, he thought the dying man was speaking of himself until he heard him tell a man standing beside the woman that he should behold his mother. When Jesus said that, the sobbing increased. It was all very confusing to Andrew, but it served to deepen his wonderment at all he was hearing.

As the morning passed toward noon, other utterances were heard from the middle cross. Included in the words Andrew heard the Nazarene say was that he was thirsty. A sponge on the end of a reed was held up by a soldier to Jesus' lips with some sort of liquid. Andrew assumed it was water, but later learned that is was not. Once again, Andrew heard the man speak.

"It is finished!"

"Do you know what the man meant by that utterance?" Andrew inquired of another onlooker who sounded like he might be someone of some education.

"Friend, I don't understand anything that is going on here. I have heard the man teach and it was always about loving your enemies and doing good for those who treat you badly."

"Then why is he being crucified?"

"I would not say this where many could hear me but, between you and me, I think the whole thing is political."

"What do you mean, 'political'?"

"Well, I think some of the uppity-up religious people who run things around here were afraid this Jesus might just have actually been the Messiah. If that were true, it would put them out of business."

Andrew became a little defensive. "Oh, I don't think that could be. My father is a priest and a very good man!"

"I beg your pardon. I didn't mean to offend, but your father must be one of the few good men. Well, I think I will go back to the city. I have had enough of this injustice!"

Shortly after the man with strong opinions left the hill, Andrew heard Jesus of Nazareth say with a strong voice, "Father, into your hands I commit my spirit!" With that, Jesus' head slumped. He was dead, but the other two prisoners still held onto life.

The Roman centurion in charge of the execution squad, having witnessed everything that took place on the hill that day, could not help himself. When Jesus died, he exclaimed, "This was truly the Son of God! This man was innocent!" Perhaps he made the statement because of his pagan superstitious beliefs, or perhaps he, at that very moment, accepted the claims made by Jesus. Andrew didn't know, but the words kept ringing in his ears as he made his way back to the city.

Jesus' words haunted his thinking for days until it drove him to begin to search the scrolls of the prophets. He had to find out for himself if one very huge mistake had been made in killing Jesus, or that the man was only another deluded would-be messiah.

At thirty-four, Andrew and the man on the cross were nearly the same age. It deeply moved him that such a person should lose his life at the peak of his manhood for no other reason than he claimed to come from God. For some strange reason, Andrew identified with the man from Nazareth, even though he had never met him or talked with him.

*

The shepherd, Lehabin, interrupted Eliab's story. "Before you go further into your story about your family and this crucified man, I meant to ask you earlier how you got the name of Marcus. That sounds gentile."

"My father, Andrew, began to serve a wealthy gentile named Marcus after he and my grandfather could no longer get along. The gentile added his name to my father's because he came to like him very much and considered him part of the family."

"That sounds very strange to me that your father, who was the son of a priest, would become like family to a gentile. Very strange indeed."

"I think I can make you understand how it happened if I can go on with my story."

"By all means! Tell your story, but don't make it too long. We want to know about Masada!"

Eliab continued to recount to the shepherds what happened after everyone left the hill of Golgatha. "You see, it was the day before the Sabbath and they all needed to go home and prepare for the day of rest. My father told me how, because of the lateness of the day, it was necessary to get the bodies off the crosses. To leave them there on the Sabbath was considered an offense to our people, so the Roman soldiers went about breaking the legs of the criminals to hasten their dying. When they came to the man from Nazareth he appeared to be dead already, but to make sure a spear was pushed into his body near his heart and it proved that he was dead, so they didn't bother to break his legs."

"Just a minute, I don't understand what breaking the legs has to do with anything."

"According to what my father told me about that day, it was because as long as the dying could push up with their legs, they could continue to breath and that meant they could sometimes live for days. So, you see, if they couldn't breath, they would die sooner."

"Now I understand. What did your father do when the crucifixion was over?"

"He told me that for a long time he just stood there on the hill and looked at the pitiful scene. He described how the sun was at the very edge of the horizon and that meant the Sabbath Day was about to begin. This was a very special Sabbath because it was the Passover Sabbath and a very solemn time for devout Jews. To leave the bodies on the crosses would have been considered a ceremonial pollution. The Jewish leaders were very anxious to have the bodies removed."

"What did they do with the dead men?"

"I don't know about two of them. Normally the Romans just let the birds and the dogs eat on the bodies, but the one called Jesus was cared for by two very important people."

"That seems very strange to me. Why would they take care of the body of a convicted criminal?"

"I don't know that either, except that the governor granted their request to bury the man. My father said one of the men was very rich. Both men were members of the Sanhedrin. They took the body from the cross and carried it to a tomb the rich man had made for himself out of solid rock. My father said that the rich man, Joseph of Arimathaea, was considered a very righteous man."

*

Eliab related more of what he had learned from his father and how Jesus may have been wrapped in burial cloth and entombed, but his enemies were not through with him. They were well aware of the rumors that had often been repeated that Jesus predicted he would live again after three days. Some thought he was referring to the rebuilding of the Temple after it would be destroyed, but many others believed he spoke of his own death and resurrection.

To be sure that there was no trickery by his disciples; such as stealing the body and claiming he was alive again, the High Priest and others arranged with the governor to have soldiers stationed at the tomb. In addition to armed guards, there was a seal placed upon the great stone that covered the opening. The Jewish leaders wanted to make sure they never heard of Jesus again.

"Is that all there was? Was that the end of the Nazarene?" "

"Oh no! Three days later the story was being told everywhere that the man from Nazareth had come forth from the dead!"

"You can't be serious!"

"I am! My father told me all about it years later. He said that the news began to spread throughout the city that the Nazarene was seen alive after he had been placed in a tomb. Even the Roman soldiers who had been sent to guard the tomb whispered of it among themselves so that their superiors could not hear them admit that a miracle had taken place. He who was dead was alive."

"You don't really believe that do you?"

"I didn't then, but my father swore that he saw Jesus himself with many of his followers not long after the report of his resurrection. I still have a hard time to accept the reality of such a thing, but my father was a very truthful man and he believed it, because he began to go through the scrolls to find out if the prophets had written about this event."

Andrew began to go often to the synagogue and take the scroll of the writings of the prophet Isaiah and carefully read what the prophet had to say about the Messiah who was to come to save Israel. He did that for weeks and it led to many discussions with his father, Abdi.

Eliab said, "It was more like arguing than discussing."

*

Andrew's thirst for an understanding of all the events surrounding the death and burial of Jesus prompted him to search for Nicodemus, the man who helped in removing the Nazarene's body from the cross. It took a few days, but he was able to find him praying in the Temple. When the man had finished his prayers, Andrew approached and asked for a moment of the teacher's time.

"Why do you want to speak with me?"

"If you could, please help me understand why you were willing to attend to the body of Jesus when other leaders hated him?"

Nicodemus took Andrew by his arm and pulled him away from others who were standing around. He took him off to a secluded corner of the courtyard and gazed forcefully into the young man's face. "Why do you want to know about such things?" It was not a question as much as a demand.

Andrew replied, "I was there on the hill when he died and his death has affected me deeply. With so many people wanting him dead, and with you being a member of the ruling body, I am amazed that you became involved with him. I need to know who this man really was."

Nicodemus looked around as if he expected someone to ask them what they were talking about. He had good reason to be wary. It was well known among the leaders that he and Joseph had asked the governor for permission to take Jesus' body from the cross and place it in a tomb. It was a very uncomfortable feeling for Nicodemus, in spite of his high standing in the community. It was that very position that caused the others of the ruling body to question his loyalty to all the accepted traditions.

"Young man, did you hear the Master's teachings?"

"No, but I wish I had. I do know that he was accused of claiming to be the long awaited Messiah, but it was unjust to put a man to death for such a claim."

"Son, you do not understand the tenacity of our leaders to uphold the rabbinical teachings."

"Oh, I think I do, teacher. My father is a priest and he does not want to even let me ask questions. I have many questions."

"Obviously, your first question is concerning the identity of the man who was killed and who now is rumored to be alive from the dead. Was he the Messiah, the Anointed One? I though so; I was convinced he was from God or he could not have done all the miracles he performed. He taught with his own authority. He did not have to quote the opinions of the great rabbis."

"Then you must have met him at some point in time before he was murdered."

"Please, young man, do not refer to his death too loudly as murder. It could go badly for you if the wrong people heard your accusation."

"Then, what would you call it?"

"Tragic, unjustified, but also divinely appointed."

"Divinely appointed! How can you say such a thing? Are you blaming God for his death?"

"It isn't a matter of blame. God is sovereign. He could have prevented the death, but Jesus' death was necessary to fulfill prophecy."

"I don't understand!"

"I can not go into all that you need to know standing here. What you must discover for yourself is found in the scrolls. Your father is a priest and you are a man. You have every right to search the scrolls for yourself. See the leader of the synagogue and ask to look at the scroll of Isaiah. Also, look in the scroll of Micah, but start with Isaiah."

"In what part of the scroll shall I begin?"

"At the beginning. Read slowly and think about what you will be reading. So many students and scribes just rush through the words so quickly, if they ever take the time to read anyone but Moses. In their haste they miss the teaching altogether."

"Teacher, I asked you if you had met Jesus before his death and you did not answer."

"Yes, I met him. I was afraid of what the other members of the Sanhedrin might say, so I went to him at night. I had learned where he often spent his nights outside of the city and I asked him how I might gain eternal life."

"You? But you are a righteous man and a teacher of the scriptures. If you do not gain eternal life, who will?"

"The Master said to me, that unless a person is born again, he cannot see the kingdom of God."

"How is it possible for a person to be born a second time?"

"That was what I asked him. It was then my eyes were opened to a great truth. I could never inherit eternal life just because I am a son of Abraham, or that I am thought of as righteous, but I needed a different kind of birth than that of the flesh. There must be a spiritual birth and that spiritual birth comes by believing in the Messiah just as the prophets presented him. He died that we might live."

"Wait a minute! This is getting far too deep for me. You have to explain what you mean."

"All the explaining I might do would not be as effective in you finding the answers to your questions than if you would honestly search for them yourself. I told you where. Now, I have lingered here as long as I dare and you have been seen with me longer than you should."

Nicodemus quickly scanned the courtyard as if to see which direction he ought to go as he pulled his robes tightly to him and hastily turned away from Andrew. He left him standing alone and more than a little perplexed.

Andrew watched Nicodemus as he turned a corner and disappeared and his mind quickly rehearsed some of the man's words. *This thing about having a spiritual birth is such a new thought to try to understand in the context of all I have been taught. Why couldn't Nicodemus just tell me if Jesus was the prophesied Messiah? I don't know much more than I did before we spoke.*

Andrew made his way down from the Temple Mount to his father's house, but Abdi was not at home. There was no use asking him the questions he needed answered. Abdi was too opposed to anything about the man from Nazareth to calmly discuss the subject. If Andrew was to know the truth, he had to do what Nicodemus suggested. He would search the sacred writings.

CHAPTER THREE

Searching for Truth

Yong Eliab Marcus told the shepherds who had rescued him how his father, Andrew, immersed himself in carefully reading the prophetic writings. The more he read the more questions he had. In Isaiah he read that when the Messiah finally appeared he would have to suffer greatly. His suffering was not to be for anything he did. In fact, when the Messiah came, his own people would hate him and reject him. As the Messiah endured his suffering, the prophet wrote that the people would turn their backs on him.

In the same portion of the scroll of Isaiah, Andrew discovered something that he could not understand. The prophet wrote, "Surely our grief he himself bore and our sorrow he carried." Did this mean that Messiah would suffer in the place of the people? The question kept racing through Andrew's mind.

Farther on in the writing, Andrew read: "He was pierced through for our transgressions." Did this correspond with the thrust of the spear into the side of the Nazarene and the spikes driven through his wrists and feet? Andrew was not ready yet to concede that it did, but the possibility compelled him to read more. "But Jehovah caused our sins to fall on him."

Andrew sat up straight as if someone had suddenly turned on a light in a very dark room. He had heard his father talk about the ritual of making sacrifices to atone for the sins of the people of Israel, such as in the Passover. In the ancient history of the Hebrews there was the sacrifice of a lamb and then the blood of that lamb was smeared upon the back of a goat. The goat was then driven out into the wilderness, probably to be killed and eaten by wild animals. The blood from the lamb being placed on the goat symbolized the taking away of the sins of the people.

Would that happen to the Messiah? Would he be sacrificed and then become, like the goat, the one to take away sin from his people? The pieces of the puzzle were beginning to fall into place, but it was not enough evidence to be utterly convincing. At this point in time, Andrew was only working on a theory. Before he could take any of his findings to his father, Abdi the priest, he had to have undeniable proof that the man who was put to death on the cross was Israel's Messiah.

Andrew had learned from his father that the men who interrogated Jesus tried to get him to confess to some crime, but the Nazarene gave not one word in his own defense in spite of all that was done to him by his accusers? Was he not also quiet, even when the Romans whipped him with the bone tipped leather thongs that ripped open his back? Andrew read, "And like a sheep before his shearers was silent, so he did not open his mouth."

A few lines farther on Andrew came across the words, "He was cut off out of the land of the living for the transgression of my people to whom the stroke was due."

Andrew stood to his feet. "It is as plain as anything can be that Messiah was meant to die for the sins of Israel, just like Jesus died!" He sat down again. What was clear to his own heart would not be clear to his father's mind. It was the mind that had to be convinced and then the heart would follow; at least that was the hope Andrew carried for Abdi.

In the days that followed his first discovery of a connection between the Messiah and Jesus, Andrew returned to unroll the scroll and pour over the words. He read again the same section of the scroll and his eyes fell on the phrases, "I will allot him a portion with the great … because he has poured out himself in death and was numbered with the transgressors; yet he himself bore the sin of many and interceded for the transgressors."

"There it is! Confirmation! Jesus was the scapegoat for us all! He bore our sins and took our punishment! What did Isaiah write? 'I will allot him a portion with the great.' The body of the Nazarene was placed in the tomb of the wealthy Joseph of Arimathea. He was given a place with the great. What is so clear to me will surely be dismissed by my father. I fear that his mind will not be open to new truth. What more can I find that might convince him?"

The hour was very late and leader of the synagogue told Andrew he had extended as much time as he could. It was well past time to close the doors. Normally such courtesy would not be given, but because he was the son of a priest Andrew was afforded a special dispensation.

"Son, I have made an exception today, but from now on, you must come at a more convenient time to examine the scrolls."

Andrew thanked Kallai and left with the notes he was able to scribble down. He planned to improve on the form of his information to make it presentable to his father and to a good friend named, Amasa. Andrew hoped he could convince Amasa of what he had discovered in the writings of Isaiah. Getting Abdi to accept the truth would be much harder. He was willfully blind to anything except traditional beliefs and interpretations.

Two days later Andrew presented his notations to Amasa. "See what I have found? See how it all goes together; what Isaiah wrote about the Messiah and what has happened to Jesus the carpenter?"

"Andrew, I can understand that you think the information parallels what the prophet wrote, but it must be a coincidence. Just as you said, this Jesus was a carpenter. He came from Galilea and Nazareth. No one of any notoriety has ever come out of that backward region. I was told that the Messiah would be from King David's home town of Bethlehem and out of the tribe of Judah. That doesn't fit the man from Nazareth."

"Well, maybe Nazareth isn't where he was born. Who might know where Jesus was born?"

"If anyone knows, old Kenaz would. He has lived long enough to know more than any other person in all Judea, but I think you are wasting your time, Eliab."

"You might be right, but I have to find out. Tomorrow, I will look for Kenza and ask him."

It took two days, but Andrew finally traced the whereabouts of the ancient one and they talked of many things. In fact, they talked of many things about which Andrew did not really want to know. It was so hard to get the old man to stop talking long enough for Andrew to ask the questions he wanted answered. Eventually the subject of the place where Jesus of Nazaeth was born was introduced.

"Why would you want to know such a thing? The man was executed by the Romans as a criminal. You should ask me about someone important."

"So, sir, you do not know where he was born."

"I didn't say that, did I? I happen to know some people who knew some other people who traveled with a man named Joseph and the young woman to which he was engaged when Emperor Augustus demanded a counting of the Jews be made so he could tax us more. They had to go all the way from Nazareth to David's town to be counted. It was over thirty years ago. The woman, who was not much more than a girl, gave birth to a son in a cattle stall while they were in Bethlehem and they named him Jesus. I suppose it was the unusual circumstances of the baby's birth that caused my friend to remember what he had been told. It may be the same Jesus, but there are many boys who have that name. Why is this so important to you?"

"I was with my father when Jesus was crucified. I remained for the whole time because I couldn't believe what was happening to the man. After all, he was a rabbi. My father refused to stay with me to observe all that took place. What I saw that day made me angry and then it made me curious to know more about the one who was crucified just because he said he was the Messiah. That, to me, didn't seem to be much of a crime. Surely it wasn't worth nailing him to a Roman cross."

Kenza placed his hand on Andrew's shoulder. "Be careful son. Do not become too curious and don't express your dissatisfaction too strongly with what our leaders have decreed. The members of the Sanhedrin are still very disturbed about how close they came to losing control of the people to the Nazarene and they may be looking for anyone who still might think the man was the promised Messiah. It might not be healthy to ask too many questions."

"I thank you for your concern and for the information, but I do have one more question. Did any of the prophets write about where Messiah would be born? A friend of mine said it was supposed to be Bethlehem. I would like to know if his information is true."

"If you can find a scroll of the prophet Micah, read it. You may find your answer there, but most rabbis and even the scribes seldom study Micah, so you may have to find someone among them who cares enough to show it to you."

Andrew became excited about the possibility that he might actually read for himself where Messiah was prophesied to be born. He ran to the synagogue to find the Kallai; the man who had helped him with the scroll of Isaiah.

"Andrew, are you wanting to study to be a scribe, or a priest like your father? You should have started when you were a young boy."

"No sir, I am just looking for information to satisfy my own desire for knowledge."

It took awhile for Kallai to search through the many scrolls in an old cupboard, but finally the scroll of Micah's writing was found underneath other more frequently used scrolls which the scribes and the rabbis favored. Andrew blew eagerly, but slowly, unrolled the scroll with great care and then began to read. A little beyond the middle of the writing he come to a portion that made his heart leap. "But as for you, Bethlehem of Ephrathah, too little to be among the clans of Judah, from you one will go forth from me to be ruler in Israel. His goings forth are from long ago, from the days of eternity."

Andrew stopped reading. He mused aloud, "What does this mean? Is it in reference to King David? No, David was not from eternity. Yet, whoever this person is, he is to rule over Israel. So, he is a king; that much I know."

After reading the same passage twice more, Andrew continued farther. "He will give them up until the time when she who is in labor has born a child. Then the remainder of his brethren will return to the sons of Israel." Andrew placed the scroll on a table and exclaimed, "This is too hard for me!"

Just then, Kallai stepped into the room to see how Andrew was doing in finding whatever it was he wanted to know. "Tell me, Andrew, have you discovered the treasure for which you so diligently search?"

"Yes and no. I found the portion in Micah that mentions part of what I want, but I am not able to understand. It is like a riddle to me."

"Let me see if I can help you." Kallai read carefully where Andrew was pointing and then looked up with a smile on his face. "You have found a reference to the Messiah who will one day come to be king over our people. He comes from God and so he will rule with divine authority."

"You say he will come some day, but he hasn't come yet, correct?"

"That is what I believe, yes."

"But what if he has come and we just did not know it was him?"

"Oh, Andrew, when he comes there will be great rejoicing and loud hosannas."

Andrew wanted to remind the leader of the synagogue that the day Jesus last came into Jerusalem the people did that very thing and they called him king, but the young man thought it best to refrain from making the connection between Messiah's reception and the one Jesus was given only a few days before he was condemned to death.

Andrew asked the leader of the synagogue to please replace the scroll among the others and thanked him for his help. He went back to his father's house and thought over everything that he had gathered, but he was not content to end his search for more truth.

Andrew, with his wife, Elisheba, lived in the same house with his father, Abdi, and his mother, Deberath. It had been a compatible arrangement until right after the crucifixion of Jesus. Now, it was becoming a house divided. Abdi was not happy with Andrew's passion to learn more about the man from Nazareth. He was afraid that people might begin to think that Andrew was one of the followers of Jesus and that it would reflect on Abdi. Other priests might even begin to question Abdi's loyalty to the traditional interpretation of the scriptures taught by the great rabbis. He feared the wrath of the members of the Sanhedrin and the high priest. It could cost him his position and reputation.

That evening, as Andrew stretched out on his bed next to Elisheba, he began to share some of his findings in the scrolls. There was one particular passage that kept coming to his mind. It was early in Isaiah's text. He remembered it was something like, "A son would be born as a gift to Israel and his names would be, Wonderful Counselor, Mighty God, Eternal Father and Prince of Peace. He would govern eternally in peace, sitting on the throne of David in justice and righteousness."

"Andrew, who would that be?"

"My love, that person is the Messiah. He is to be born as a man, but he is also deity as seen in the names by which he is called."

"But husband, how can a man be Jehovah? God is Spirit!"

"I do not know, but there it was in Isaiah. The Messiah is born as a human baby, yet he is divine. But we know that there is only one God. I keep coming back to Jesus with everything I have read. Even the centurion at the cross believed that Jesus was the Son of God. I do not know what the soldier meant by his words, but Son of God to us is a title of the Messiah."

Elisheba place a gentle hand on Andrew's arm. "What does your father think about this?"

"I am afraid to mention anything more about what I am doing at the synagogue. He is already upset. But I remember another thing I read in Isaiah. It was about Jehovah giving a sign to our people. 'A virgin will bear a child, a son, and he is to be named Immanuel.' I asked Kallai what was the literal meaning of that name and he said it means God is among us."

As the two lay in the dark and contemplated the passages, Andrew rose up on one elbow as if something had just dawned on his mind. "Those passages are in agreement! Jehovah wants to awaken our people to him by coming to us to draw our people back to faith. A son, born miraculously without the curse of sin upon him, is to save our people from our transgressions and rule us in peace as God himself!"

"Andrew, that is too radical! If you talk to people about what you have just concluded, they will brand you as a blasphemer and have you stoned to death!"

Andrew got out of bed and went to the open window. The night air was cool and a slight breeze wafted across his face as he struggled with his thoughts. The clear sky was filled with stars and everything was so quiet Andrew could hear his heart pounding as he wrestled with his knew convictions. "Elisheba, how can I live with myself if I deny such truth? How can I turn my back on all that I have discovered and keep my self-respect?"

Elisheba slipped from beneath the bed covering and joined her husband at the window. She held him tightly from behind and placed her head against his shoulders. "Dare you go find this Jesus who is supposed to be alive from the dead and ask him who he really is?"

"Bless you, my love, I must! In the morning I will try to mix with the crowds and listen to what people are saying. Perhaps I may hear a rumor of where he might be. I know that his disciples had been in hiding for days, but someone must know something."

On the next day, while it was early, Andrew made his way into the heart of the city and browsed the markets. He pretended to be nothing more than a shopper as he inspected the vegetables and wares being offered for sale. Two men sat on stone steps near one of the merchants' stalls and spoke in very low tones, but Andrew was able to hear enough to realize that there was to be a gathering of certain men in Galilee.

By the manner in which the two men spoke it was obvious they were trying to guard the information. But how was Andrew to know of whom they spoke? It could be any number of persons. There were many unhappy factions in Israel. Some just grumbled about conditions, but others were militant and dangerous.

Andrew decided to follow the two men when they left the market area. They went down several narrow streets and then suddenly vanished. Andrew began to hurry to try to catch a glimpse of the men and, as he rounded a corner, he met them face to face.

The larger of the two men sternly asked, "Why are you following us? Who do you represent?"

"I admit I was following you, but I only represent myself!"

The shorter man looked intently at Andrew. "Did I see you among the people at the crucifixion? You were with another man and I recognized by his garments that he was a priest. Are you spying on us?"

"No! I am not spying, and yes, I was with a priest. He is my father. I have been greatly troubled over the crucifixion of Jesus. If you are followers of the Jesus, I want to see him."

"What makes you think we are his followers? And why would the son of a priest want to see a man who is supposed to be dead; a man despised and rejected by the religious leaders?"

Andrew was becoming very nervous. Perhaps these men were not who he assumed they were and he might be in trouble if they were not followers. "I heard you mention Galilee and I know Jesus spent a lot of his ministry in that region. I have been researching the scrolls of Isaiah and I have come to suspect that a great mistake was made by our religious leaders."

"I would not say that too loudly if I were you. It would not be healthy if the wrong people heard you make such an accusation. So, young man, what conclusion have you reached about Jesus?"

"If you are not who I hope you are, I could wish I had not said this, but I believe that he is the Messiah, the Son of God, but I need to have my conviction verified or I will never have peace in my heart."

"You said your father is a priest; how does he feel about your belief?"

"He doesn't know all I have discovered, but he is very upset that I have been asking questions. We are of opposite opinions. He follows the thinking of the Sadducees that there is no life after this life and therefore Jesus is dead and there is no resurrection. I believe the rumors that Jesus lives and I must meet him!"

"Are you married?"

"Yes."

"How does your wife believe?"

"Elisheba accepts what I have concluded."

The two men motioned for Andrew to stay where he was standing as they walked away several feet and conferred between them. They returned to Andrew and gave him warning. "We have to be very careful.

The political atmosphere around her is too hot and we are going away for awhile. If you are serious and you are not lying to us, make arrangements to meet us in Bethany tomorrow at noon by the well. We will be watching for you. If you are alone and we feel it is safe, we will take you north with us to Galilee. But if we do not think it is safe, you will not see us. Is that understood?"

"Yes! I will be there. Thank you!" Andrew turned around to leave and then turned back to ask another question, but the men were nowhere in sight.

As instructed, Andrew made arrangements to be away from home for what could be a few weeks. It was a long walk to Galilee. Elisheba was asked not to tell where he was going, but just that he had many things to do that would keep him occupied away from Jerusalem. That explanation would never satisfy his father, but it would have to suffice until Andrew returned.

Andrew waited at the well in Bethany as he had been told to do. It was high noon and the air was very warm. He sought some relief under a nearby scraggly acacia tree, the leaves of which gave very little protection from the rays of the sun. He waited for nearly an hour before the men he was to meet approached him. One came from the north and the other from the south.

The large man by the name of Mahath greeted Andrew. "I see you have kept your word to come here by yourself. Are you prepared for a long journey in search of the truth?"

"Indeed, I am. And I am very anxious to get started. Could you please tell me how long you have been a follower of the Messiah?"

Mahath hesitated to give a direct answer. "A short while. It was the visible resurrection that convinced me of who Jesus is."

"So, you are not one of the men who traveled with Jesus before he was arrested."

"No, we are not of the inner circle of disciples, but that doesn't matter. He treats us all as brothers. Take a drink from the well and let us cross over the Jordan into Perea and then north along the east side of the river. It is a little longer than going through Samaria, but I think we will have less trouble with those who may be looking for the Master's disciples. We will keep going until we reach Capernaum on the north coast of the Sea of Galilee."

"And how long do you think it will take us?"

"Perhaps five or six days. It depends on whether you are a good walker."

"You lead and I will follow."

The men chuckled, "We said the same thing to Jesus."

＊

The three men arrived at Tabor on Friday. They rested there on the south end of the Sea of Galilee over the Sabbath and moved on around the lake on Sunday. From Tabor to Capernaum they followed the west shore by way of Tiberias, Magdala, and Gennesaret. As Andrew and his companions approached Capernaum they saw a group of men huddled around a small fire on the shore. Mahath and his friend picked up the pace. They knew the group had to be brothers in the faith with the Master in their midst. He would be teaching them as well as fellowshipping with his men.

Peter saw the three men coming toward the gathering and went out to greet them. "Brothers, who is that with you?"

"Another Andrew; he and your brother ought to get along very well."

There was a moment of laughter and then Peter became more serious. "What do you know about this man?"

"Only what he has told us, but we were very careful. He comes with a great desire to have what he believes about the Master be confirmed."

"And, pray tell, Andrew what do you believe?"

"I believe that Jesus is the Christ, the Son of the Living God."

"Those words are very familiar to me, almost as if I had said them myself some time ago. And what will it take to confirm your belief?"

"I want to see Jesus!"

"Andrew, would you believe even if you would not see the Master?"

"I would, but my father would not. I must have the proof I need to convince him. At this point, he is quite upset with my investigations."

31

"What investigations?"

"I have been reading the scrolls of Isaiah and Micah about the promised Messiah and have come to the conclusion that Jesus is the one about whom they wrote."

"Indeed, that is the truth. It took some of us a long time to realize that, even though we lived with him. Will your father not believe your words?"

"No. He is a priest and as stubborn a man as ever lived. For him it is all tradition and rituals. When I face him again I want to be able to tell him I saw the resurrected Jesus!"

"Do you think he will believe your testimony?"

"Perhaps. I do not know, but meeting the Messiah will surely affirm my faith."

"Then, come and see for yourself."

Andrew didn't know what to expect. He had never seen Jesus up close. His view was of a man dying on a cross, but as Andrew entered the group he immediately knew which man was the Master. He was common enough in his features, but there was something about his eyes and his smile that drew Andrew to Jesus.

The Master saw in the mind of this man the seed of a great faith, but he also saw that there were still doubts. "Andrew, you have come on a long journey to have your soul satisfied. You have come in search of truth. I am the Truth whom the Father has sent and you want proof of that, do you not?"

"Yes, Master. I need proof if I am to tell others what I have found."

"If you have the proof you seek, that I am who I am, what will you do with it?"

"I will do whatever you tell me to do."

"Will you teach the truth to your son?"

"Master, I have no son."

"You will have. Will you teach him the truth?"

"Yes, I will."

"Then come see the imprint of the nails in my wrists and feet. Touch them if you wish."

"I see and I believe! I need no other proof."

"You, just like Thomas, are blessed because you have seen and believed, but there will be many who come later, after I have returned to the Father, who will be blessed because they believe even though they have not seen with their eyes what you have."

*

Andrew spent several days with the Lord Jesus and his men, but it was time for them all to begin a slow journey back south. Their destination was the Mount of Olives. To return to the vicinity of Jerusalem was a risk for the followers of Christ. It had only been four weeks since the excitement of the crucifixion and the news of the resurrection. But the Master had plans for himself and his band of brothers.

There were many others who had seen Jesus in that period of time. Hundreds heard him speak again of the kingdom of God and his promise to return again to gather those who believe. Until Jesus returned as King, certain things would have to happen. The plan for the ages was about to begin a rapid unfolding, starting at the Mount of Olives.

CHAPTER FOUR

A House Divided

Young Eliab Marcus asked for more water as he paused in his account of what his father told him of meeting with Jesus in Galileee years before the boy was born. Andrew had returned to Jerusalem from the north fully convinced that Jesus was the Messiah of whom the prophets had written.

"Son," said the chief shepherd, "you say your father went from Jerusalem to the Sea of Galilee to find the man from Nazareth. And you say that he see actually saw Jesus?"

"He told me that he saw Jesus, spoke with him, and even ate with him. My father, Andrew, listened to the man he called the Master and his teaching of a future kingdom of everlasting peace."

"Did you believe what your father said?"

"I could not believe that my father would ever lie to me and yet it was difficult to accept, because grandfather Abdi spoke against the whole story. He told me my father was confused. As a priest, grandfather Abdi was well informed of the traditions of our people. I wanted to believe my father, but I found it hard, because I had not seen those things for myself."

*

Jesus of Nazareth was, for many, the Messiah and Savior. He led his primary disciples, along with a few others, back from Galilee to the vicinity of Jerusalem. It was a bold move on his part. There were many powerful people who could not afford to have it known that Jesus was still alive, nor did they want to believe it themselves. The story they circulated as a cover for the reports that the Nazarene had risen from the grave the third day just as he had predicted, was that the disciples had stolen the body and hidden it somewhere. The Roman guards at the garden tomb knew the truth but money, along with the threat of summary executive for having fallen asleep while on duty, sealed their lips.

For safety reasons, Jesus had told his men he would meet them in Galilee. They needed protection from the possible rounding up of those who supported the Messiah. Now, after nearly forty days of appearances in many places, Jesus led his men up the mountain east of Jerusalem. It was time to give them their last instructions and leave the planet temporarily.

Andrew stood back several feet from the disciples, who were known as Apostles, and listened to the words of his Lord. First, Jesus reminded the men that he had all authority from the Father. This authority was both in heaven and on earth. Because he had this power, his second statement was a commissioning of the Apostles, and all his followers, to go make other disciples from every nation on earth. Jesus entrusted the authority he had to them to bring others to saving faith in the name of the Father, Son, and Holy Spirit.

It was the first time that Andrew had heard the mention of the Holy Spirit. Through his research he had come to believe there was a unity of Father and Son, but now he found out that there was a third member of that unified godhead. Oh, Andrew knew his father's priestly blood would boil with rage at such an idea. How would he ever be able to convey this tri-unity of God to Abdi?

Included in the marching orders of this small band of believers was the charge to teach people all that Jesus did and said. The Messiah concluded his commissioning with the promise that he would be with them always; even to the end of the world. How Jesus could be absent and present at the same time was something Andrew would eventually come to understand, but for the present it was a mystery to him.

The power for the followers of Christ to be able to obey the Messiah's commands would come, Jesus said, "When the Holy Spirit has come upon you, Begin in Jerusalem and then go to all Judea and Samaria. Go everywhere with my message and the hope of eternal life and tell people even in the very remotest places."

When the Messiah finished speaking he began to rise up from the earth and slowly ascend into the sky until brightly shining clouds formed and obscured him from view. All of the followers stood there gazing into the sky as though they were transfixed. Nothing like this had ever been seen before. There was hesitation as what to do next. The followers were astonished! It could be said they were stunned until two men dressed in brilliant white appeared and demanded to know why everyone was staring into the heavens. These men declared that Jesus would return one day in the very same manner in which they had just seen him go. Andrew knew Abdi would never accept that he had seen angels. Abdi and the Sadducees did not believe in angels, even though the Hebrew Scriptures mentioned them often.

When the men in white vanished it was like an awakening. With the words of Jesus and the promises of the men, who must have been angels, still ringing in their ears and filling their hearts, the Apostles and others obeyed and went back into the city in spite of the danger. They gathered in a large upper room where they had met many times before and began to pray. Andrew was one of the one hundred-twenty souls who spent the next ten days praying and waiting for God's power to be bestowed upon them so that they could have the courage and boldness it would take to follow the Lord's Mount of Olives orders.

During the Upper Room prayer experience, an unheard of phenomenon occurred. As the believers prayed and praised, visible droplets like fire came from nowhere and alighted on each person without burning their skin or sourcing anyone's hair. As one body the followers of the Messiah filed out of the meeting place and into the street to begin to spread out among the crowds of people that swelled Jerusalem's population at the time of the feast of Pentecost. Divinely empowered, the believers moved among the masses and each began to witness of their faith in Jesus as the Savior and the Messiah, not only of Israel, but of all mankind.

Jews and converts to Judaism from all over the known world were gathered in Jerusalem and the surrounding area to celebrate Pentecost, the second of the three great festivals of Israel. Pentecost, or "the fiftieth," had to do with the offering of the first fruits of a sheaf of grain during The Feast of the Unleavened Bread. It was observed fifty days after the celebration of Passover. On such special observances people slept wherever there was an open space. The hillsides around Jerusalem became camping grounds for the worshippers.

Because many who made the pilgrimage to the Holy City were from more than a dozen different countries with more than a dozen different languages, sharing the good news of God's gift of salvation would be an extremely difficult, if not impossible task for Jesus' people, except for the fact that they were empowered from God to speak to each person so that each person heard the message in his or her native language.

The impact of untutored Palestinian Jews sharing the story of Jesus in languages the witnesses had never known caused an eruption of excitement. The power of the resurrected Jesus in the lives of his followers brought great conviction of sin and great expressions of saving faith so that on the day of Pentecost more than three thousands souls were added to the assemblage of believers whom the Lord had called out of darkness into the eternal light of the Living Truth: the Messiah.

Many of Christ's followers were spontaneously reminded that he had said, "I am the Way, the Truth, and the Life; no one comes to the Father, except by me." In the days following the spiritual breakthrough on that glorious Sunday, other converts were being added to the body of the faithful.

*

Lehabin, the shepherd, interrupted Eliab's story. "Just wait a minute! Do you expect me to believe that ordinary Jews, many of them from the area of Galilee, actually began to speak in languages not their own; languages they had never learned? You are a boy with a huge imagination, or you are one big liar!"

Eliab exclaimed, "I am not a liar! My grandfather read to me from the Scripture that lying lips are an abomination to God! I am telling you what my father told me. He didn't know why it happened or how. It just happened. You don't have to believe it! Let me go on with what I have to say or let me go to sleep, but if I go to sleep, I can't tell you about what happened on Masada."

"All right! But hurry and get on with it!"

"My father became a member of the growing number of Jews who were turning to faith in the Messiah. They were spoken of as the 'called out ones.' Father's trouble really began, he said, when he had to tell my grandfather what he discovered in the scrolls and that he met the risen Jesus. They argued often: sometimes for hours. Of course, I did not know about those earlier family conditions. I wasn't born until my father was fifty-seven years old. Jesus had told him he would have a son, but it took another twenty-four years after the promise before my mother gave birth to me. My grandfather was eighty-two and he was so happy to have a grandson."

"That is very old. Your grandfather, Abdi, must have been too feeble to enjoy you when you were small."

"Not so. I spent a great deal of time with him. He hoped I would become a priest, like him. It was from about age five to age ten that I found myself in the middle between my father's faith in the Messiah and my grandfather's angry refusal to believe that Jesus had risen from the dead and ascended to heaven. He was especially upset when there was any talk of the Messiah coming back a second time."

Eliab went on to relate to the people sitting around him that meals became explosive times because his parents and grandparents lived in the same house. Andrew would begin to offer a prayer of thanks for the food on the table and that was all right until it came to the end of the prayer when his father said he was praying in the name of Jesus.

Andrew begged for peace, but also for tolerance of his faith. "Father, I do not wish to be argumentative, but there are certain facts that cannot be denied. You have also heard of how Jesus healed people's sicknesses, like blindness and paralysis. Only God could do that!"

"Lies and rumors; nothing more!"

"No, father, too many people were present when some of these things happened; like the man who was lame from birth and could not even move himself into the Bethsada pool near the Sheep Gate. All Jesus did was speak and the man was able to walk for the first time."

"Nonsense! It was a trick of some kind! You were not there. How do you know of this?"

"I have met people who were there and they swear it is the truth! It was prophesied that when Messiah came he would give sight to the blind and the lame would walk. Can you not see that this scripture is fulfilled in Jesus?"

"Stop! Stop immediately! You blaspheme and you do it right to my face and in my house! I forbid that you ever speak that name again in my hearing!"

Such events were repeated. Andrew was willing to stand up for what he believed was his right to pray in the name of the God who came to earth to bring life and light to people who walked in darkness, but Abdi believed that he had the truth and it did not include the man from Nazareth. To Abdi, Jesus was a myth, a fraud, and he was also dead. After death there was nothing. He could not stand to hear Andrew speak of the hope of a life in heaven.

Grandmother Daberath warned Abdi many times that if he didn't stop being so angry his rage would cause his death, but it seemed like Abdi loved his hatred of the name of Jesus more than he loved his only son. Andrew tried many times to reason with his father, but the conclusions to which Abdi clung were not based on reason or on any tangible evidence. Everything was based on the traditions which were long established by the respected rabbinical teachers. If fact and tradition clashed, tradition always won.

A few days after the Pentecost experience, when Christ's followers made such an impact on the streets of Jerusalem, Andrew grew brave enough to approach Abdi to lay out again to the older man what Isaiah had written about the Messiah, but Abdi refused to listen.

"Father, please, if you disagree with what I have concluded from the prophet's statements, at least let me tell you what has happened to me in the last few months."

The old priest motioned for Andrew to be seated. "I will listen as long as you refrain from pushing this messiah of yours in my face."

"Sir, it is not pushing. It is sharing experiences."

"Get on with it, but be careful!"

Andrew told of his chance meeting with two of Jesus' followers who, at first, did not trust him, but finally were willing to include him in a journey north into Galilee and to the region near Capernaum where he met the risen Jesus.

"I warned you to not bring up fables about the man!"

"Father, please, I am not making up a fable. Look at my face. Would I deliberately lie to you? I am you only son."

Disgustedly Abdi replied, "Tell your story and be done with it!"

"He was gathered with a few of his closest disciples and they were talking about the Kingdom of God; how one day it will come and there will be peace."

"And he let you join in the discussion?" The words were spoken with sarcasm.

"A big man named, Peter, asked the Teacher if I could have some proof that this person, whom you don't wish to be named, is the very one who was crucified and this person you don't wish to be named showed me the nail prints in his wrists and feet. He was not a spirit. He was flesh and blood!"

"My foolish son, you believed what you saw, but you did not see what you think you saw."

"Father, I am a grown man and have a wife. I am a man who deals with merchandise; buying and selling. I am not a fool that I would be so easily duped to believe a fake messiah. You continue to disrespect me because I have come to an understanding about this Jesus that you will not accept for no other reason than he did not fit into your presumptions. You reject both the prophet's words and my own experience!"

Abdi struggled to his feet. "Enough! I have heard enough of your babbling! You say I have disrespected you. Well, you have broken the commandment to honor your father and mother! This is a house divided! It is my house and it will be as I say! I will have no more of this Nazarene mentioned between these walls! This messiah of yours has brought a sword between father and son!"

Andrew told his father that he read in the scroll of Isaiah that the messiah was of the root of David and that the Messiah was referred to as a root out of a dry ground, indicating that when the Anointed One appeared he would not come from a prominent place, but rather from a most unlikely one. Andrew came to the conclusion that Nazareth was that dry ground and the virgin named Mary was from that obscure place. For Andrew, Jesus fulfilled the prophecy.

"Father, I honor you in everything except in this matter of rejecting the One who has given me a life of peace with Jehovah and a purpose for living. You are right. This is a house divided. Elisheba and I will find another place to live so that there can be peace between you and me."

Abdi shook his garment in great anger. His eyes bulged because of his rage. "There can be no peace between you and me as long as you deny the traditions and follow after that man!"

With great sadness, Andrew withdrew from his father's presence and told Elisheba of the impasse that made it impossible for them to stay under the roof that was owned by Abdi. "I will go and ask Marcus, my employer, if he knows of a place where we can stay until it is possible to build a house of our own."

When Daberath learned that the split in the family had led to her son and daughter-in-law moving out of the house, she begged her husband and her son to reconcile, but the rift was too wide and too fresh. It would take time to heal, if healing was even possible.

The Merchant, Marcus, responded to Andrew's need for living quarters by making available to him a small house on the edge of his larger complex of buildings. "It is yours for as long as you need it, Andrew. It will also make it possible for you to become more involved with the inner workings of my business as a manager. I have no children and my wife is too old to bear a child, so if you and I can get along as well in the future as we have so far, who knows; this business my become yours one day."

*

A few years passed and Andrew became a very good businessman trading in goods from all over the lands north and east of Israel. He gained a great deal of business for Marcus and in the process accumulated considerable wealth for himself. Andrew and his father passed each other on the street, but never entered the other man's house. Abdi watched from a distance as his son became well off. He fought against the thought that his son's prosperity might be a blessing from God.

Andrew's father became aware that his son contributed a large amount of his money to the growing community of those who believed in the man they considered Jehovah in human form, but of course, the Nazarene was never seen. His disciples believed him to be alive from the dead, but in heaven awaiting a time for him to return to earth. Abdi scoffed and fumed at such notions. As far as he was concerned the Nazarene corrupted the faith of the Hebrew people. For that he had deserved to die.

Andrew, on the other hand, was convinced beyond all doubt that Jesus was the fulfillment of all the hopes of Israel as prophesied in the sacred scrolls. There was an ocean of differences between father and son and so it was easy for Andrew to drift ever closer in his relationship to the gentile, Marcus. Andrew was the son of Abdi after the flesh, but emotionally he was more the son of Marcus.

The assembly of believers in Jerusalem grew so quickly that problems also grew. There were many widows who had no support. There were families that needed income. Providing food for such a diverse mass of people, who often had only their faith in the Messiah as their common bond, was a serious issue. During the rule of Emperor Claudius a famine struck the land and compounded the problem of caring for the members of the Jerusalem fellowship. It fell to people like Andrew to give large portions of their wealth to care for fellow believers who had little or nothing.

Andrew became good friends with a man named Stephen; an articulate and learned follower who was elected by the believers to help govern the daily affairs and needs of the congregation scattered throughout Jerusalem. So effective was Stephen in persuading people of the truth concerning Jesus that the leaders of the Jews plotted to get rid of him, as if the death of one man would stop what the Spirit of God was doing to bring people from darkness to light.

A band of conspirators found Stephen while he was witnessing within the city. They laid hands on him and carried him out to a place where they proceeded to denounce him as a blasphemer. They judged him worthy of death by stoning. The group of men began casting large rocks on the believer and, as he was dying from the repeated wounding of his head and body, the man testified to the glory of God and his spirit left his body to join with Jesus in heaven.

Andrew came upon the scene just as the final blow was struck and saw, in spite of the blood, a face shining with the presence of God's Spirit. Standing to the side there was a young man whose garment indicated he was a Pharisee. He seemed to be standing guard over the cloaks of the murderers and agreeing with their action. Andrew was horrified and thought, *How can people who pretend to be so righteous justify so horrible a deed?*

*

While there was a growing resistance to the burgeoning Messianic believers by the leaders of the Jews, there was also an intensification of unrest and hostility between Jews and Romans. Two decades after Jesus arose from the dead emperor Claudius banned Jews from Rome and sent several thousand able bodied Jews into military service in the western parts of the Empire. This ban was not fully enforced, but it was a portending of the deterioration between Jews and Romans.

Four years before Nero took power in Rome and ten years before General Titus marched against Jerusalem, Andrew and Elisheba welcomed a son into their family. Jesus had promised Andrew he would have a son, but there were times when he was ready to give up hope. It was nearly more than two decades of waiting and praying.

Elisheba was several years younger than Andrew but drawing near the end of her time for bearing children. Eliab brought a renewal of enthusiasm into the home. His arrival also brought Abdi and Deberath back into the life of their son and daughter-in-law. A truce was declared between father and son so that Abdi could enjoy his grandson.

For a short time, all went well. However, it was not long until a tug of war over Eliab began. By the time he was four years old, Abdi was driving a wedge between Andrew and his small son.

By the end of the rule of Claudius Caesar, life in Israel had become pressure-packed because the Jews were in such disfavor. Rome was tightening its grip on conquered lands; especially the land of the Jews. In addition to the long term hatred between Rome and the Jews there was the controversy over the followers of Christ who was spreading throughout the empire. In particular, there was a former Pharisee, Saul of Tarsus, who appeared in Roman courts under accusation by the religious leadership of Judaism. There were riots in many places where he preached Christ to the masses. Saul, who became known as Paul, was in and out of prison for his beliefs. The anger of the Chief Priest and others was hot against him.

Between the spreading movement of Christ-followers and the constant hit and run tactics of Zealots against Roman soldiers and Roman interests, the ire of Rome was growing toward all Jews and the followers of the man named Jesus. When Nero became Caesar, his hatred for both groups exceeded that of his predecessors. Hatred led to persecution. Greater restrictions were placed on Jewish self rule and people chaffed under the oppressive measures applied by their conquerors.

In this atmosphere, Abdi became more and more agitated, first against the Romans and then against anyone with whom he might have reason to find fault. Andrew felt the brunt of his father's anxieties. Abdi wanted to wrestle Eliab away from Andrew's Messianic influences. Soon, because of the frequent suggestions to Eliab that his father was being unfaithful to Judaism and that he was wrong in his beliefs about the Messiah and Jewish laws, Eliab began to resist Andrew's teaching and often quoted Abdi as his authority.

CHAPTER FIVE
Genocide in Jerusalem

As Eliab recalled his story of what he knew of the family tension between his father and grandfather, Lehabin interrupted. "Don't you think you should be ashamed to have been so disrespectful to your father?"

"I did not at the time. I was too young to realize how much my grandfather Abdi disliked my father."

The boy was growing very weary of telling about how his family was torn apart by rivalry, hatred, and religious differences, but his new friends urged him to reveal more. They had become interested in the drama. He recalled the last words he heard the grandfather say to Eliab's father before the family became divided.

"You are no longer my son! To me and my house, you are as dead!"

Living apart from Abdi and his antagonism toward the followers of Jesus, Andrew was able to take many homeless, hungry believers into his own new and larger house and provide for them. He also allowed his home to be used as a meeting place where the Apostles would gather to teach and to fellowship with new converts. There was a great expense involved, but Andrew felt it was his mission from God to do all that he could for the growing movement.

The day came when the merchant, Marcus, was no longer able to run his business. His age and health made it impossible to oversee his own affairs. Marcus called for Andrew to come to his house. He had something very important to tell him.

"Andrew, you have been faithful to me in everything you have done. By your hard work you doubled my business and income. Now it is time for me to let go and turn it all over to you."

"To me? I am not a relative. We are not even of the same race. You are a Roman and I am a Jew! I do not understand."

"We are both men. You, Andrew, are as close to being a relative as I have. If I have any kin, I know not who they are or where in the empire they might live. No, son, what I have I give to you. In fact, I give you my name. I will make it legal by Roman law and with it goes citizenship. Roman citizenship may come in very handy for you one day, or for your son. From now on you are Andrew son of Marcus!"

Andrew was overwhelmed and no amount of objections to his employer's generosity would change Marcus from the course he had set. Andrew, having lost any standing in Abdi's household, now had a position and more wealth than he could have ever imagined. Now, he could do even more for the spiritual family to which he also belonged. "Marvelous are the ways of the Lord!" Andrew said often.

With the war clouds gathering on the horizon and rumors flying that the Romans might attack Jerusalem, Andrew thought it best to relocate his wife and child, along with his newly acquired business, to Lydda nearer the coast of the Great Sea where there was more commerce along the coastal trade routes. The family that Andrew had known since birth was beyond repair and his first thought was for the safety of Elisheba and Eliab.

*

Eliab continued telling his story to the shepherds, "At first I resented my parents for making the move to Lydda, but I made new friends. However, I never accepted the faith of my parents. It was difficult for each of us."

"So you are orthodox?"

"No. I am a Zealot. I love Israel but I am not religious. I am a fighter against the Romans and will be until I die."

"Those are very big words for a small man. How do you think you will fight the Romans all by yourself?"

The boy, wanting so hard to be a man, bristled as he reacted to the doubt being expressed. "There must be more like me! I will find them and we will make the Romans pay for their crimes against our people!"

"Well, my young warrior, we have heard that there is a gathering of a few rebels north of here beyond the Jabbok River at a place called Amathus. It is an area where the Romans have not yet sent troops because there are few people living there and too many places where soldiers can be ambushed and then the attackers disappear quickly."

"That is where I will go."

"Not until you fulfill your promise to explain what happened at Masada."

*

Eliab requested another drink of water to sooth his throat. "When I was ten years old we heard that the Romans were gathering forces in the north of Israel and were ready to march to Jerusalem, but they were also massing legions along the coast and the troops would be taking slaves of our people as they moved inland toward Jerusalem. My father believed it would be best to go back to Jerusalem where there were walls to protect us. Many people had the same hope and the city was crowded. The Zealots wanted to make a stand against the invaders, but there were far too few trained Jewish fighters for the number of Romans they would have to face."

Lehabin smirked, "Did not anyone realize that all the Romans had to do was starve out the inhabitants?"

"Everyone sadly realized that fact after the food and water was used. Sickness and lack of anything to eat took many lives, yet the people stubbornly refused to surrender. When the soldiers began to scale the walls which had been badly battered for many weeks, thousands of the people committed suicide. Those who had the strength to stand their ground were systematically slaughtered or taken for slaves."

Eliab recounted how the enemy soldiers methodically went from street to street, passageway to passageway, house to house, and business to business throughout Jerusalem as they worked their way up to the

Temple Mount. It didn't matter if it was an old man, a woman, a child, the crippled, or the sickly.

The Roman legions were very proficient with spears and the short broad sword. When the Zealots realized the hopelessness of the situation, they were able to find ways out of the city. After that, there was little or no resistance. Death came quickly and efficiently. It was brutal beyond belief. The cobblestone streets ran with Jewish blood.

The Romans vented their hatred for the Jews and gave vent to the malice that had built up over the years. There was no effort to spare a soul. In the eyes of the unconscionable Roman soldier, to kill a Jew was of no more consideration than the severing of the head of some unwanted vermin.

Lehabin wanted to know, "What happened to your parents and how did you escape?"

"The last I saw of my parents, they were in the Court of the Women at the Temple. I could hardly believe what I saw. My father stood beside my blind and feeble ninety-six year old grandfather who was sitting on the ground because he could not stand from the effects of age and hunger. They were trying to protect my mother and several other women as the soldiers came running at them from across the court, stepping over many bodies to reach my family. Although my father and grandfather had not been able to live together because of the differences in their beliefs, they were side by side when the soldiers attacked them. I did not see them die, but I know it had to have been swift."

Eliab paused for a moment. Recalling the circumstances of those last seconds of terror in Jerusalem caused his emotions to well up momentarily. "I was grabbed from behind by two men who took me away from the Temple and into a very narrow passageway that led to an underground chamber. From that chamber we squeezed into a very narrow crevasse in the rock foundations of the city. We hid there for three days and then made our way at night back to the surface beyond the city walls."

"Who were your rescuers?"

"Zealots. That is how I ended up at Masada. Before my new friends took me far to the south, we hid out for several days in different places to avoid being captured. We watched from a distance as our most sacred place of worship was torn down stone by stone. As the great building blocks came smashing down they crushed everything, including the streets upon which they landed. Those gigantic stones became rubble so that the only thing left was one foundation wall. My father had told me that the man he called the Messiah predicted that the temple would be destroyed, but few believed it was possible."

"So, you say you went south with the Zealots. Is that how you arrived at Masada?"

"Yes. After the Temple was destroyed the Zealots took me with them and we traveled only in the very early hours of the morning or the dusk hours of the evening and collected other survivors along the way down through the rugged area where King Saul had pursued David and his men. We went through the pass to Engedi from the plateau of Tekoa where the prophet Amos had lived. Eventually, we arrived at the base of the great rock fortress that had been occupied by Roman Legions who were no longer there."

"And how did you get your education about Masada?"

"From Eleazar, our leader. He said that the legions were needed elsewhere at the beginning of the war against Israel and we were able to occupy the rock. The Romans had left Masada four years before they attacked Jerusalem."

"And now, little man, are you ready to tell us what happened when the Romans returned to the rock?"

Eliab hung his head and his eyes became watery. "Death happened! After nine months of trying to starve us out, the Romans had completed a ramp of earth high enough to assault the wall and break through. All that they were going to find were bodies. A suicide agreement among the people left the Romans with nothing over which to gloat. The people stole the victory away from the enemy. Eleazar commanded that I be spared and let down by rope from Masada. He charged me with telling the story and so I have. Now, Lehabin, please let me sleep."

"You could have already been sleeping if you hadn't taken so long to tell us your story."

Eliab slept fitfully in spite of his exhaustion. It was well passed sunup before Lehabin awakened him to give him food and water. "When you have eaten, you must choose whether to stay with me and be a shepherd or follow your wish to join with the Zealots. If you go with them, you may not live very long. The Romans are determined to wipe out every one of them."

"I have already made my choice. I must fight on behalf of those who died at Masada."

"Since that is what you wish, I will prepare some dried goat meat and a goat bladder of water for your journey."

By mid morning Eliab had thanked his benefactor and said his goodbyes. He started north over the rugged landscape east of the Jordan, yet close enough to the river that there was cover for him in case he came across anyone whom he felt might not be someone he could trust. On the third day, Eliab came to the Jabbok and crossed over to a rocky piece of ground where he made camp for the night before approaching Amathus on the next day.

At first light, the boy who had escaped two massacres in a period of three years nervously moved toward the town. As he emerged from behind a stand of stunted trees strong hands grabbed him and placed a large knife against his throat. A voice barked, "Don't kill him, he is just a boy!"

A short muscular man in his thirties stepped from behind the trees. "It is all right Uzal, you can let go of him. What are you doing sneaking around like a little thief?"

"I am no thief! How do I know you are not thieves?"

"You have a smart tongue, boy."

"Let me thrash him, Judah!"

"No, Uzal, he needs to tell us why he is all alone out here. Where did you come from and where are your parents?"

"My parents died in Jerusalem when the Romans came. I have been with the Zealots at Masada."

"Why are you not still with them, then?"

"They are all dead, that is why!"

Uzal looked at his leader, "Judah, his story smells like a rotted goat."

"Yes, Uzal, it sounds like a lie, but let us learn more from this great big Zealot."

"Do not mock me! I alone was allowed to escape. I would have rather died with all of them!"

"They are dead? All of them? Eleazar also?"

"Yes, him also. When it became hopeless, Eleazar ordered certain men to make sure people committed suicide. During that night, I was let down from the rock part of the way and was able to climb down to the desert and slip through the Roman lines."

Judah roughly grabbed Eliab's right shoulder, "How long ago was that?"

"I have lost the number of days, but I think it had been ten or maybe twelve."

"So why are you here in this place?"

"I was kept from dying of thirst and hunger by some shepherds three days south of here and they told me I might find some rebels near Amathus. Are you who I am looking for?"

Judah and Uzal walked Eliab back into the shade of the trees and they sat on the ground. Judah wanted to know why this boy wanted to join with a band of Zealots and so Eliab explained that he hated the Romans and wanted to avenge his parents and grandparents, as well as all those who were murdered in Jerusalem and those who died on Masada.

"You seem to have a great amount of hatred for being so young. How good are you at fighting?"

Eliab shook his head, "I do not know, but I want to find out."

Judah decided to allow Eliab to stay with his small band of rebels for a few days, but he was not willing to take him in as a fighter. He was not willing to risk the lives of any of his men who would have to protect an inexperienced boy.

After three days, Eliab was given supplies and told it would be best for him to cross over Jordan to the west and then travel northwest to a town called Dothan. There was a group of refugees from Jerusalem who had set up camp near there. He could be there in two days. Judah believed there would be few Romans in the area and they would not pay any attention to a boy even if he should come across some soldiers.

"Just in case, if you see a group of Roman soldiers, stay far away from them and don't look at them. Keep you head down. Never look a Roman in his eyes. They hate for Jews to do that."

Eliab was able to reach Dothan without any trouble by following the advice of Judah. Only once did he see a squad of soldiers and they paid him no attention. Near the edge of Dothan Eliab saw someone he thought he knew and approached a woman with four children huddled together around a small fire. The woman was cooking some vegetables in a pot. The boy stopped and stared at a girl about his own age. She lifted her head and looked back at him. This girl was a picture of loveliness with her dark hair cascading over her shoulders framing her brown eyes and her smooth olive tan complexion. For a moment, the young man only stared.

"Eliab! Is that you?"

"Rebekah?

"Yes, it is I! Eliab, we thought you were dead!"

"I came very close to death more than once."

Rebekah inquired, "Where have you been?"

"Masada."

"Masada? Word has spread that all died there!"

"Not all. I will tell you about it later. Do you have a morsel to spare? I am very hungry."

"Of course! Mother, come see who is here. It is Eliab Marcus!"

The next two days were spent with Rebekah and her mother. The father, Kedemah, had died in a raid by the Romans, but the family escaped before the attack and had been moving from place to place every few weeks. When they arrived at Dothan it seemed to be a safe area and so they had remained for the past two months.

Eliab wanted to know where he could find some fighters. He wanted to join the Zealots again. He was told that the action was in the north between Tiberias and Hazor, but the rebels would retreat to Gadara on the east side of the Jordan after each raid. That was where Eliab decided he would go. Rebekah and her mother pleaded with the boy to stay with them and not become mixed up with the Zealots.

Rebekah revealed to Eliab that she and her family had become followers of the Messiah and had been scattered from Jerusalem a year before the Romans sacked the city. They fled because of heavy persecution by the leaders of Judaism.

"Oh, Eliab, you cannot imagine what we believers have endured after the death of Deacon Stephen. Your father saw that wonderful man murdered, but in those early days your father's Roman citizenship gave him protection that our family did not have. Did you know that you have citizenship in the empire through your father."

"I despise it and I renounce it!"

"Can you do that?"

"I don't know, but I hate everything about Rome!"

Rebekah's mother, Lois, urged, "Son, the Messiah would not want us to hate even our enemies."

Eliab bristled at the idea. "I can not accept that! The Romans killed my parents and grandparents! They killed your husband, how can you not hate them?"

Lois reached out and placed a hand on Eliab's arm. "They crucified our Savior, but he forgave them."

The boy pulled away and impolitely rejected the woman's effort to persuade him to remain with her and the small group of Christ-followers. Eliab rejected the idea. "You do what you want, but I believe in an eye for an eye!"

Rather than argue with Eliab, who was so adamant in his desire to get revenge, Lois fed the boy and gave him shelter under their tent until the next day when he gathered his meager belongings and bade farewell as he turned his face east again in the direction of the caves of Gadara.

Eliab, son of Andrew, whose bestowed gentile sir name was Marcus, rationed his meager supply of food and water as he traveled northeast toward the juncture of the Jordan River and the Yarmuk tributary. Crossing the Jordon was going to be very difficult because of the steep fall of the river that was cut deeply through the limestone gorge. It took two full days of cautious travel to arrive at the west bank of the Jordon where Eliab decided to rest over night and look for a way to cross the next morning.

The boy, who wanted to be a fighter with the Zealots against the Romans, was jolted awake just as dawn was breaking. "Wake up, Jew!"

Eliab sat up and rubbed his eyes. Standing around him were six soldiers with short swords drawn. "What do you want with me?"

"Check his belongings for anything useful!"

A soldier rummaged through the sack in which Eliab had his food and water. "He has something one might call food if you have no care for what you eat. There is a small skin filled with fluid. I assume it is water."

The soldier in charge wanted to know why Eliab was camping out all by himself. "Are you part of a group, or on your way to join a band of thieves?"

"Sir, my parents are dead, as are all my relatives. I am just wandering from place to place hoping I might find someone who could use a servant."

The skeptical officer retorted, "For some reason, that story just does not seem true. How old are you?"

"Thirteen, sir."

One of the other soldiers spoke up. "He is just a boy and not a very big one either. We have bigger fish to fry if we can locate the hideout of those Zealots."

The officer agreed. "All right. We better not waste our time with minnows. We will head east to the other side of Jordan. The rumor is a band of rebels might be near Gadara. If we find them, we will wait until it is dark and then attack the camp. Trophimus, tell the others what we are planning and have them meet us at the mouth of the Yarmuk. As for you boy, go west to Nain. You might find someone who needs a skinny child to feed pigs."

"Good one, sir! A Jew feeding pigs!" The soldiers all had a hearty laugh as they moved out toward the Jordan."

As soon as the Romans rounded a small hill and were out of sight, Eliab grabbed his sack and began running north to out flank the soldiers. He wanted to cross the river north of the point where the Romans planned their crossing. He was determined to find the rebels before the soldiers did and alert them to the danger.

Young legs and a stout heart made Eliab a swift runner and, whenever the ground was suitable, he put that skill to good use. The soldiers were in no hurry. It was a job to find and kill Zealots and it would get down when it got done.

The young Jewish boy, who by his own thinking and the traditions of his people was a man, was on a mission. He had to locate the Zealots first. Eliab found a narrow enough gap in the lime stone that was gouged out by the Jordan where, with a good run, he could leap to the east bank. He barely made it and clawed his way up the steeply sloping ground to a place where he could stand. From this crossing point, he began to run directly east. He knew that the Yarmuk flowed in a southwest direction and he would be able to intersect it due west of Gadara.

Just before Eliab reached the tributary he rounded a rise in the terrain and came face to face with three extremely mean looking men. He was exhausted from running and was in no condition to deal with one grown man, let alone three. The boy stood still and waited to see what was going to happen to him.

"Where are you going in such a hurry, boy?"

All Eliab could say was, "The Romans are coming! The Romans are coming!"

CHAPTER SIX
Young Zealots

Having been confronted by the rebels Eliab attempted to warn them of danger from Roman soldiers scouring the area, His effort to convey the information was doubted. The largest and ugliest of the three heavily bearded men demanded, "What makes you think there are any Romans around here?"

Defiantly Eliab replied, "I saw them! In fact, I heard them say they thought there were rebels near Gadara and I came to spread the warning!"

A Zealot with a long diagonal scar on his left cheek challenged, "How do we know you are not a spy for the Romans?"

Still trying to act braver than he was the boy shot back, "And, sir, how do I know that you are not a Roman dressed like you are so you can catch rebels like me?"

The air was filled with deep bass laughter. "Men, we have a smart boy here who has an even smarter mouth! Just who are you and from where have you come? And what makes you a rebel?"

"I am Eliab, son of Andrew, who was son of Abdi the priest."

Sarcastically the leader retorted, "That is some pedigree you have. And, where are your parents? Should you not be at home doing chores?"

"My parents are dead! Murdered by the godless Romans in Jerusalem three years ago!"

"So, that is why you want to be a Zealot?"

"Yes! I want to spill the blood of as many Romans as I can!"

The large man looked at his companions. "This little fellow wants revenge. Well, we want that and a whole lot more. We want freedom." Justus looked back at Eliab as he started to walk a way. "Do you also want freedom for our people?"

Eliab stiffened his neck and spoke slowly for emphasis. "If killing Romans brings us freedom, then yes! But I need to find the rebels and warn them of the Roman soldiers' plan. They are crossing the Jordan at the Yarmuk and marching toward Gadara!"

"How many?"

"I saw six, but there are more I did not see."

Justus spoke to his men. "Probably a cohort in reserve. We need to set a trap for them."

The leader of the band of rebels and his men turned and began to hurry back to their encampment. Justus stopped and motioned to Eliab, "Well, boy, if you want to be a Zealot, come on!" Eliab's heart leaped. At last he would be able to have a part in paying back the Romans for what they did in Jerusalem and Masada.

Five miles farther on, Justus made a sound. It was a signal and it was repeated from someone that could not be seen. Soon a dozen men, most of them young and rugged looking, emerged from behind rocks. They joined with the smaller group led by Justus and continued on another mile until they came to a rise in the ground that was guarded by huge boulders. Up on the high ground Eliab saw another two dozen men. All together, the Rebels numbered a few more than forty.

Justus gathered his young rebels around him and explained what he had learned from Eliab. "We have to trust that this young fellow is telling us the truth. We will deploy our fighters and conceal ourselves among the rocks. Five of you will go west and wait until you see the Romans coming. Make sure they see you and then run back here. Lead them to this open area and the rest of us will wait in ambush."

A rebel sounded a note of caution. "But Justus, we are no match for a cohort of professional soldiers."

"You are right; we cannot stand and fight, but we can hit and run.

When the Romans are gathered, each one of you will throw two spears. Aim well! The suddenness of our attack will cause the Romans to pause long enough for us to escape. Since they will not see how many there are of us, they may not give chase immediately. The rocks will cover our retreat."

Another rebel questioned, "Where do we go from this place after the attack?"

"Omar will take half of you east toward Abila. The rest of you will go with me north to Hippos just east of the Sea of Galilee. Omar, when you are sure you have eluded the Romans, circle north and then west and rejoin the rest of us in the hills east of Hippos."

The five young men who were to play the part of the bait to catch the Roman fish hurriedly left their companions and began walking west toward the Jordan River. They stopped about a mile from the place where the trap was to be sprung and waited out of sight. An hour passed before they heard the sounds of marching. The heavy sandals of the Roman soldiers thumped against the ground. Each rebel's pulse rate quickened as he made ready to dangle the live bait before their enemy.

Uzal, the leader of the five rebels who were to act as bait, stepped out of concealment into the open. He stood and watched as the Romans came closer. A soldier pointed to him and called a halt to the column. At that moment, the other four rebels stepped into the line of sight. Having been clearly seen, the five Jewish young men turned away and began to run. It was clear to the leader of the column that the Jews had weapons and a signal was given to attempt to chase them down.

Thinking that there were no more than the five Jews, the soldiers abandoned caution as they sought to make the capture. The pursuers began to shorten the distance between them. The rebels suddenly swerved to the right and started up the steep grade leading to the open area between the boulders. At the far side of the open ground the five turned around with their backs to the rocks. This action emboldened the Romans to rush them for a quick kill and, as they approached, a flight of spears launched by the full rebel force silently pierced their targets.

As the soldiers tried to recover from the surprising assault, several of the second shower of spears found unprotected flesh while others glanced off of shields. The soldiers who were still making their way up to the high ground suddenly found many of their companions lying dead and wounded while others were reeling backward. The whole scene was one of confusion. By the time the Romans had regrouped and began to encircle the place of the ambush the rebels had disappeared.

The young zealots and their leader, Justus, divided into two groups as they had planned and put as much distances between themselves and the soldiers as they could in the first half hour. One rebel from each group lagged behind as a lookout to make sure they were not being pursued. Should the lookout see the Romans coming, he was to race ahead and give a warning to the others.

Although the attack was successful and the rebels made a clean get away, the anger and hatred of the Roman soldiers was many times hotter than it had been. What had been just a job to find and kill rebels was now a mission of revenge. No doubt, there would be some innocent people who would taste the bloodthirstiness of the Romans as they scoured the country east of the Jordan in search of the Zealots.

Omar's group spent just one night near Abila. They acquired supplies and then began an arcing march east for half a day and then north for the following day before turning back to the west with the intention of joining up with Justus and his men. Unknown to Omar, the other group had to flee into the desert east of Hippos because of a scout group in-force of Romans who were searching the east bank of the Sea of Galilee and all the towns in the area. Runners had been sent from Garada to alert the Legions stationed near Tiberias concerning the ambush and killing of several soldiers.

While Justus took his fifteen men well wide of the area near the Sea of Galilee, in the direction of a northern territory known as Gaulanitis, Omar was walking right into the teeth of the Roman sweep. He and his men stumbled into a nest of soldiers and had no chance to run. Although they fought valiantly to the last man, they were no match for an enemy trained in the art of war and hardened by combat in various parts of the empire. Fortunately for Eliab, he was in the group led by Justus that had escaped detection and was wandering about over an open wilderness plateau.

Justus was unaware of what had happened to the others of his band of Zealots. If he was to be effective, he needed to recruit additional followers who had a passion for inflicting pain and death upon the Roman conquerors. After a month of hiding and living off of whatever they could scavenge, beg, or steal, Justus led his young men north to Raphana. He took Eliab with him into the village while the rest of the rebels remained hidden just south of any dwellings. He and Eliab would pass themselves off as a father and son looking for work.

There did not seem to be anyone who would hire a worker and most of the inhabitants were suspicious of people they did not know. On the Sabbath day the two wanderers went to the synagogue. The building was very small and attended by a handful of elderly men.

Justus inquired of the lack of young men. "I see men my age and older, but no one my son's age. What has happened here?"

Rakem, leader of the synagogue, answered, "Who might you be asking such a question. You are not from around here?"

"I am Justus and this is my son, Eliab. We are survivors of the persecution. I am surprised to find a synagogue in this area."

"We are also survivors. We came here three years ago and built this gathering place. All of our young men are away during the day and only return at night to be with their families."

"That seems strange. Are they looking for work?"

Rakem proudly announced, "They are looking for other young men who are willing to stand against the Romans."

This news gladdened Justus and he inquired, "Have they been successful?"

"They have gathered only a half dozen. Together they add up to twenty who are willing, but not very able. They have no leader and no one to train them how to fight against soldiers."

Justus asked, "What is your name, sir?"

"I am Rakem, leader of the synagogue. We have no rabbi. You look like a strong man. Could you advise us what we should do?"

The deep and hearty laugh that characterized the rebel leader surprised everyone. "Jehovah has smiled on you and me. I have just over a dozen fighters south of the village. We have killed many Romans, but our number is not large enough presently to be on the attack. If your young men have a real passion against our enemies, I can train them how to fight a certain way that brings results without having to stand up against large numbers of soldiers."

Rakem felt that God had answered his prayer. "Bring your men into the village a little before dark and we will find them a place to rest and get food. Tomorrow you and I will discuss what it is that you seek to do to make fighters out of shepherds."

Justus and his men, along with the twenty from the region around Raphana, spent the next six months practicing throwing javelins, becoming more accurate with slings, and learning the proper methods of using the Roman short swords which had been stolen from supply depots. It was also important to learn to employ the strategy and tactics of a rebel force that could strike fast and escape.

There had to be safe locations to which they could retreat to after a raid. That required traveling to such places in advance and storing supplies. It would soon be time to test the skill of the combined band of rebels in the use of hit and run tactics where the advantage was on the side of the rebels. The rule was to never attack a superior force where there was no suitable way to escape.

The rebel leader felt satisfied that his motley gathering of young men were ready to be tested. Playing war in the wilderness plateau region north of the Sea of Galilee was now over. It was time for action. But before any fighting, there had to be a target scouted and plans rehearsed. Justus and two of his more experienced men armed only with small concealed knives crossed over to the west side of the Jordan five miles north of where it fed into the Sea of Galilee from the highlands. Their destination was Chorazin which was located two miles inland from the sea coast town of Capernaum.

Chorazin was a small town in the hills. It was populated by a people who showed little faith in Jehovah, even though there was a synagogue. There had been no exhibition of belief in the man Eliab's father believed to be the Messiah of Israel. Justus felt it would be a location he and his band of Zealots could use as a temporary re-supply place following a raid farther down the coast of Galilee.

The three Zealots made their way south from Chorazin, making sure to stay west of the populated areas until they arrived in the hills above Tiberias. King Herod Antipas built the city and named it after a Roman emperor. Herod made Tiberias his capital for administering the provinces of Galilee and Perea. Because of Herod's desecration of tombs in order to have the land he wanted for the city, Jews who were strict in their religion avoided Tiberias until Jerusalem was destroyed by the Romans and the Jews were forced to scatter. When Justus and his companions arrived to scout out an opportunity to cause the Romans pain, Tiberias was not yet known as the center for Rabbinical teaching that it later became.

Roman soldiers were encamped at various locations outside of Tiberias. It was the rebels' responsibility to discover which was the least defended and most vulnerable to an attack. There had to be an easy way to escape the area before other soldiers could be summoned. After a day of wandering around the edges of the city, it was determined that a small outpost to the north side afforded the best target. The rebels watched the camp for three days to gain an understanding of the soldiers' routine.

By the third day of observing the camp, it was clear that most of the soldiers left at mid morning each day and patrolled the coastline of the Sea of Galilee to the north and then returned in the late afternoon. That meant they could not go father than Gennesaret, or approximately six miles before they would return to their post. Any attack would have to be when the patrol was at its most northern distance. That would give the rebels time to make their assault, kill those soldiers still at the post, and take all the weapons and supplies they could carry before having to make a getaway.

Just to make sure the plan for escape was doable, Justus led his scouting group south from Tiberias toward Nain near Mount Tabor. From there they went northwest to Nazareth and then Cana while keeping the mountains between themselves and the Roman legions near the Sea of Galilee. If the Romans followed the trail that would be left, they would be going south while the rebels were making a turn back north to Chorazin.

And, if the Romans realized that the rebels were making a circle back north, it would be a race to see who would reach Chorazin first. Justus planned to hide water and food supplies north of that town so that his men could retrieve them quickly before crossing back over into the high plateau. Justus knew the Roman soldiers were used to long marches and could go all day without rest, but he did not know how much stamina his young men had gained in the month of preparation. Especially, he did not know if Eliab could keep up with the others. In a few days, they would gain the answer.

*

The raid of the Roman camp came as a total surprise to those soldiers who were left behind as guards. Justus and his band of fighters remained hidden until they knew the scouting patrol was near the extreme north of their march. The rebels silently moved in from all sides and caught their enemy unprepared.

It was a quick fight, Javelins did the work from a reasonable distance and then swords finished the wounded. Two of the rebels sustained slashes to their upper arms, but none were wounded badly enough that they could not manage the retreat. Swords, shields, and edible stores were taken hastily. There was no time to linger. The last act before leaving the Roman camp was to set fire to everything that would burn. Although the smoke might be seen from a long distance, the fire would be out before the patrol could make its way back to the camp.

When the Romans saw their dead companions and the destroyed camp they were spurred by rage to pursue the Zealots, but it would take time before they could determine the exact trail to follow. The immediate evidence indicated a southern escape along the Jordan. The soldiers were anticipating a crossing over the Jordan to the east and into the mountainous region from Gadara down toward Pella. For this reason, the trackers did not expect a turn to the west and so they did not look for a trail going around the southern base of Mount Tabor.

By the time the Romans realized their mistake and had backtracked to where Justus and his men took a westward turn, the Zealots had already skirted Tabor and were moving north toward Nazareth and Cana. It was now predictable that the rebels would reach their hidden supplies before a runner could race to spread the word along the coast of the Sea of Galilee, so that other troops stationed as far as Capernaum could begin looking for the raiders. Chalk up another success to Justus' leadership.

Over the next four years the Zealots gave the Roman garrisons dotted through the land a great many defeats. None were large, but they were not meant to be standard battles. By moving from one area to another and striking at places distant from the previous raids, the Romans thought there were many more rebels groups that actually existed.

Eliab had proven his worth. Although he had drawn Roman blood on just a few of the raids, he was useful in setting the fire that destroyed the soldier's supplies. He also proved he was very capable of keeping up with the older fighters and carrying his share of the stolen equipment and food.

Justus patted Eliab on the shoulder and encouraged him. "You are doing well, young man. The day will come when you will spill more Roman blood. Do not be too anxious for the next battle."

"I need to learn to throw the spear better. Mine seem to fall short."

His leader and mentor replied, "It is not easy for any of us to hit the target every time. Judging the arc of the flight comes with experience. I have watched you grow stronger as you have gotten older. Each time we retreat to a safe place, you will practice more and soon you will be our best warrior."

Eliab puffed out his chest; "Good! I want to be the very best!"

*

Following another raid, Justus led his men across the upper Jordan and deep into the interior beyond the inhabited areas thirty miles east of Lake Hula. He felt certain the Romans would not venture that far away from the normally traveled routes from Galilee to Caesarea Philippi which was far to the north. Caesarea was a well fortified Roman enclave. The rebels were sure to avoid approaching the vicinity of that city. The problem with hiding in the wilderness was that the rebels wanted to be attacking Romans instead of looking at a landscape of sand and rock.

After a month of seclusion which allowed the wounded men to recover, it was again time for Justus and Eliab to venture back to civilization to look for another target.

The same scenario was repeated a dozen times over the next three years. Justus' band of Zealots was gaining a reputation from Ashkelon in the south to Hazor in the north. Wherever there was a target the rebels found it. They especially rejoiced when they set a trap for the soldiers who were in pursuit. The bounty on the heads of the group was high enough that they could no longer trust anyone; not even their fellow Jews. The rebels were considered by some as no longer freedom fighters, but murderers and thieves who were just serving their own ends and not the welfare of the average Jew.

Instead of things getting better, the hatred by the Romans for the Zealots was being taken out on the people and this caused many to stop supporting the Zealots with food and shelter. While other rebels would continue the struggle, it was time for Justus and his men to face the reality that the power of Rome and the reach of its legions were far too great.

The decision was made to disband the rebel group and each person merge back into the population. Eliab was now going on twenty-four years of age and his experiences caused people to think of him as being older. He had no marketable trade through which he could support himself, and after a few months of wandering and doing odd jobs, he returned to Dothan where he had spent some time years before. It was there he found employment as a helper of a smith, tending the forge and learning how to work metal and make implements of various kinds.

One day Eliab was on his way to the town well with a donkey carrying two barrels to fill with water for the ironsmith's business. As he approached the well, Eliab noticed a girl who looked very familiar. When she turned toward him, he realized it was Rebekah. She had changed. She was no longer the little girl he had known before the fall of Jerusalem. She was a young woman nearly his age.

"Rebekah, is that you?"

"Do I know you, sir?"

"It is me, Eliab. Has it been that long that you do not remember me?

Rebekah, it has been many years since the Romans killed my parents in Jerusalem. I was thirteen when I escaped from Masada. You recall my visit here a few years ago, do you not?"

"Oh, Eliab, you have become so much more of a man since I last saw you! I can hardly believe it is you. Where have you been? What have you been doing?"

The young man hesitated to say it out loud for fear that the wrong person might hear him. "I have been here and there. Most of the time I was making life difficult for the Roman soldiers. Before I say anything more, are you still a follower of Jesus?"

"Yes, of course. Eliab, have you become a follower?"

"Oh, no, I have been with a band of Zealots on both sides of the Jordan, but it is time to rest for awhile."

"Only for awhile?"

"I think so. The fight for freedom and to avenge my parents will go on until the Romans leave our land."

Rebekah hung her head and stared at the ground. "I was hoping you were ready for a normal life."

Eliab scowled, "There is no such thing as a 'normal life' as long as we have invaders in our land!"

The beautiful young woman looked Eliab directly eye to eye. "Peace does not come by the absence of Romans. Peace is found as a gift from the Messiah and it is inside of a believer, regardless of what is happening around us."

Eliab really did not want to engage in such a conversation. He took a bucket and began to fill the barrels tied to the back of the donkey. The young woman could only stand and watch as Eliab ignored her declaration of a peace that the world cannot know. Her claim was being silently rebuffed.

With her hands one her hips in a posture of disgust, Rebekah made a challenge, "So, you are man enough to fight the Romans, but you cannot stand face to face with a woman and discuss how you can be released from your hatred. If you will not listen to what I have to say about the Messiah, then perhaps you will listen to the wisdom of the proverbs, 'Do not boast about tomorrow, for you do not know what a day may bring.'"

Eliab was not interested in Jewish proverbs either and turned his back on Rebekah. He was a man now, not a boy. He was experienced in the ways of a fighting man and proud of his exploits. But the young woman was not finished with her recitation. She stepped around the animal to face Eliab. "'Let another praise you and not your own mouth; a stranger, and not your own lips. Wrath is cruel, anger is overwhelming.'"

"Rebekah, I like you. I have always liked you since we first met and I want to be a friend to you, but this thing about the man from Nazareth tore my family apart and now it seems like it is a wall between us."

"Eliab, there does not have to be. We can still be friends, but I will always be a follower of the Messiah. I come to the well each day at this time. Perhaps we will meet again some day." With that, Rebekah picked up her large pitcher of water and left Eliab to his task and his thoughts.

There was a yearning in his heart for this dark haired beauty, but he felt that the die had been cast for him. He would fight against the Romans until he died and if that meant he had to forfeit the normal life of a wife and children, then so be it. That is what his head said, but his heart was not fully in agreement. Over the course of the next several days he purposely found the opportunity to occasionally make his way to the well. Eliab hoped he might speak with Rebekah about things other than religion and politics. On those few mornings when he and the young woman arrived at the same time, neither felt comfortable with general conversation.

Rebekah was deeply into her faith in the Messiah and Eliab was passionate for retribution for the death of his parents. When she tried to talk about family, it only underscored the fact that he was the last of his family. When Rebekah spoke of the future and her hope for the Messiah's return, he found nothing comforting in her words. In Eliab's thinking, the future for him was only continued conflict and probably death in battle.

Like his grandfather, Eliab had no vision of a life beyond the grave. It saddened the girl to see how hopeless he was. If God's Spirit could touch the young man's heart and change him, perhaps there was the possibility of a life together for them in Dothan.

The two young people could not share the feelings they had for each other. A wall existed through which neither could pass. The barrier was built mainly of Eliab's hatred and feelings of revenge. He also carried memories of the family conflict in his heart. Was the Nazarene who his father Andrew believed him to be, or was grandfather Abdi correct; that Jesus was a false messiah who had become the victim of his own misguided ideas?

Three weeks after Eliab and Rebekah first met at the well, she invited him to her home to meet her mother again. It was a bold move on her part and not in keeping with traditions, but in her new life as a follower of Christ she and others like her had felt freer to transgress man made rules. Her intention was to expose Eliab to the deep faith her mother carried in her heart. Perhaps if he saw her mother's joy, even though the Romans had killed her husband, it might soften the young man's attitude to the point that he would be willing to at least discuss the salvation and forgiveness to be found in Jesus.

Eliab accepted the invitation and arrived washed and looking his best. He knew that the food on the table Lois had prepared was provided sacrificially. He partook of it sparingly and politely resisted the urging of Rebekah's mother to eat more.

Lois inquired of Eliab, "Are you planning to stay in Dothan and make a home for yourself?"

Eliab glanced across the table to Rebekah and then answered without looking directly at her mother. "I have not made any plans for the immediate future. The Romans are still looking for the small band of Zealots with which I had cast my lot for awhile. My friends have all scattered, but I hope someday to join another resistance movement to drive out the enemy."

Lois' next comment was to try to help the young man face reality. "My, that is going to be a very huge task, seeing how strong the Romans are and how few Jews there are who are able to fight against them. Could you not find peace within yourself and let God sort out what to do with the Romans?"

Eliab felt like he wanted to shout his answer, but kept his emotions under control. "Honored lady, my parents were slaughtered like sheep and I find that I cannot rest until I have avenged their deaths."

"But Eliab, how many deaths will in take to satisfy your pain? Our Lord was cruelly sacrificed, but he forgave the people for what they did to him."

His voice began to sound very tense as Eliab tried to control his answer. "My father said he was on the hill when the Nazarene was crucified and he heard him say those words. I suppose that had something to do with why my father became a believer, but I am not my father! Please excuse my attitude. I am being impolite and I do not want to have you think badly of me."

"Eliab, Rebekah and I take no offense. We are able to understand your pain. We have felt it ourselves, but we also know that when Jehovah wills it, we will see our loved once again in Paradise. I pray that one day you will realize that hope for yourself."

When Eliab made his way back to the smith's shop and climbed into the loft where he had a bed of straw, Lois' words kept repeating in his mind until he finally fell asleep. As he slept, his dreams took him back to Masada and then to his rescue by the shepherds. He twitched and moaned as he relived the raids he and his Zealot friends had made against the Roman camps. Suddenly, Eliab awakened and sat up sweating.

There was a war going on inside him. He felt he was being pulled in two directions and the tension of it robbed him of any further sleep. For the balance of the night he thought of his parents and the struggle that had taken place in the family because of the different attitudes about Jesus. He also thought of Rebekah and her mother. How could they possibly be at rest after suffering the loss of a husband and father? Which did Eliab want most; vengeance, or a heart at peace with God? He didn't know: not yet.

*

Because of an informant's report to the Roman legions headquarters at Caesarea Philippi, a cohort of soldiers numbering 600 men began to sweep the villages and towns between Chorazin in the north and

Antipatris in the south and from the coastal plain to the Jordan River. The object was to locate any male Jew who might fall into the profile of recruits for the Zealots. The region covered by the sweep was Galilee and Samaria.

The soldiers began in the north and systematically worked their way toward the south by dividing the cohort into ten squads of sixty men. Word raced ahead of the Romans and young men in the wake of the sweep fled across Jordan into the regions of Decapolis and Perea, while middle aged men chose to stay with their families until the last possible moment and then hide out in the mountains that made up the spine of Israel. If they avoided being captured, the men would return to their families once the squads had moved beyond their homes.

The news reached Dothan that the Romans were about to enter Samaria. That meant Eliab had to find a place to hide. It was too late to reach the Jordan before a squad arrived on the outskirts of Dothan. This reality caused Eliab to head directly south to stay ahead of the Roman soldiers who would be moving slowly and in a methodical manner as they examined every house and business structure. They interrogated the inhabitants of each village. If they suspected someone was lying to the interrogators, that person was subject to a summary beating and lashing in order to force whoever it was to divulge information on the whereabouts of the village men. There was an obvious absence of able bodied males throughout the region.

Eliab made his way to Mount Gerizim on the southern edge of Samaria; not far from Sychar where Andrew Marcus had told is son how Jesus had broken with all tradition and social norms by befriending a Samaritan woman. It was anathema for a Jew, especially a rabbi, to even speak with a woman of Samaria. The woman he befriended was an outcast among her own people, yet Jesus led her to believe in him as the Messiah. Eliab remembered his father's story as he sought refuge among the rocks on the mountainside.

Back in Dothan, the squad of soldiers began going through the village. Every house was entered. Every temporary pavilion that housed refuges was examined and people were gathered in the center of the village and ordered to reveal information as to the whereabouts of the missing men. No one would say anything and that led to stronger measures.

The village smith, a man past fighting age, was singled out for questioning in front of everyone. Trophimus, the leader of his squad, attempted to intimidate the village smith whose name was Maadai by standing against him nose to nose and demanding an answer. "You know everyone in the area because of the work you do, so tells me where the other men are hiding or where they went! Make it quick or you will feel the lash on your back."

Maadai stood tall and straight and silent. Repeated efforts to elicit an answer produce no results and Trophimus nodded to three of his men who grabbed the smith and tore off his garment: making him stand in humiliation before the women and children. His hands were bound and tied to an upright piece of wood on the well. Maadai's feet and legs were pulled back and separated so that he was leaning heavily by his chest and head against the post.

"You have one last opportunity to escape the punishment that follows my command. Tell me where the others are!"

There was a moment of silence and then the squad leader nodded to a large, muscular soldier who held a lash that was made up of several strands of leather and each strand tipped with a small piece of bone. The sound of the lash cutting through the air was all that was heard until there was a collective gasp from the gathered crowd. The next sound was a crack and then a thud as the lash found flesh. Again and again the sickening act was repeated until Maadai's legs buckled and he slumped into a most unnatural position.

An aged man on a single crooked crutch shuffled on crippled legs as he stumbled forward through the ring of people to show himself to Trophimus. The Roman looked at the pitiful sight before him and inquired if he had information. "Will you tell me what I need to know?"

"I will tell you this, Roman; you slaughtered my wife and children in Jerusalem and left me with a body of little use! What I have to say to you is where you can go to spend an eternity with the damned and with your master, Baal-Zebub!"

Trophimus gave the old man a hard back of his hand and knocked the cripple to the ground. The nearest soldier then made one quick slash with his broad sword and silenced him forever as women screamed and began to sob while wrapping scarves around their children's faces to shield them from the horrible scene. Maadai met the same fate as the old crippled man.

"You people are on notice! We will be back through your village in a few days. By then you will choose to tell me what I want to know or your village and everyone in it will be destroyed!" With that warning ringing in the ears of the people, the squad of Roman soldiers formed and began to move farther south in their search for able men who might be sympathetic to the Zealots.

CHAPTER SEVEN

Not Even Love

Eliab Marcus ensconced himself amid several large boulders on the west upper face of Mount Gerizim. He had enough supplies for five days. If the searching Romans had not cleared from his area by then, he could hold out another three days, but hunger and thirst would force him to venture out to look for a re-supply of his necessities. He needed to stay strong in order to survive and to fight if that became his lot. For the time being, all he could do was wait.

When the sun began to die on the western horizon and slowly "descend" into the distant Mediterranean Sea, Eliab began to reflect upon his short life. He had known a good life as the small son of a godly father who was a wealthy merchant. That life changed when the Romans began their push to drive the Jews into exile. When he approached his teen years, the affluence of his parents faded. Safety was the most important issue and life really began to change. What good was a big house and luxuries if the Romans were determined to tax his father out of business? What good was a life of ease if it could not be enjoyed?

Longing thoughts of those years when he had no cares and did not need to hide in the hills like a criminal consumed Eliab's mind. Of course, to Rome he was a criminal, but he was not according to how he saw his circumstances. He was a patriot. His status came about because someone did not wish him to be murdered when General Titus and his legions attacked Jerusalem. It was for that reason he found himself numbered with the Zealots at Masada and afterward with Justus and his young men. Those associations fed his passion to have blood for blood in an effort to give him some peace of mind over the death of his parents. But, was hiding out on a mountain side like an animal the answer?

Eliab was beginning to yearn for some sort of normalcy in his life. He wanted to be part of a family, not just one of a group of raiders and pillagers. He could be caught and killed and no one would ever know. He didn't have anyone who cared what happened to him, except Rebekah and her mother, Lois. He wasn't absolutely sure how much they might be thinking of him. They were the only people he knew who might have him on their minds. Perhaps they were praying to Jehovah to spare him. The young man shook his head as though in doing so he might drive away the thoughts that prompted his feelings of loneliness.

Over the following several months Eliab's existence was reduced to scavenging like an animal and stealing what he needed in order to stay alive. He felt the emptiness that having no family and no companions brought to him. On the last few occasions when he had the nerve to venture into inhabited areas, he did not find the presence of squads of soldiers. He decided that it was time to return to Dothan and find Rebekah. She was the nearest person to being a true friend he had.

On the journey back north the young man was careful to watch for any sign of soldiers. It was apparent that the Romans had withdrawn back to their base encampments. They had flushed out a few rebels, but most had found refuge in areas not bothered by the legions. There was no way for most people to know that Rome was having problems governing the far flung fringes of the Empire and was required, because of that, to reassign forces from Israel to cope with potential hot spots elsewhere. There was still a sizeable force in the land of the Jews, but the planned sweeps for Zealots were terminated in favor of intermittent efforts to coerce the vulnerable population into revealing the whereabouts of the most militant trouble makers.

The Romans had not forgotten the people of Dothan. It had been six months since the killing of the old crippled man and the village smith. People felt the danger was passed and a few made there way back to the village, but most remained in the hills. One morning the soldiers returned and destroyed most of the inhabitable structures.

As Eliab approached Dothan he immediately realized the place looked different than when he left months before. There were a few rebuilt structures and temporary fabric pavilions. He made his way to find the smith for whom he had worked, but Maadai was not in his place of business. The forge, or what was left of it, was cold. There did not seem to be any signs of recent activity. From the forge, Eliab went directly to where Rebekah and Lois had made a place for themselves on the edge of town, but they were not there.

As Eliab stood and pondered the situation and worried about his friends and his former employer, an elderly woman came out from behind one of the ruined houses. She started to shuffle back to her hiding place, but Eliab stopped her, "What has happened here and where are the mother and daughter who used to occupy this spot?"

Hesitatingly, the beleaguered woman answered. "The Romans came looking for anyone who might be strong enough to resist them. Lois and her daughter went into the hills after the smith was murdered in front of everyone. As the soldiers left, their leader said they would return and destroy Dothan, so most of the people were living in the hills when the soldiers came back. They did much damage as you can see. It was just three weeks ago, but we have been afraid to return to our homes. I stayed because I and those like me are too old to go wondering around out there where the others are."

Eliab tried to assure the frightened woman. "I don't think the soldiers will come back here after what they have done. I must go find Lois and Rebekah. If I locate others, I will encourage them to come back to Dothan."

In a few days, Eliab was able to not only find his friends, but several of the other town's people. Eventually more of the former residents began to repopulate the community. Eliab took over the forge and made it his own place to live and work. He became the new smith. He had watched and assisted Maadai long enough that he could do some of the basic work of a smith. He would improve with experience.

On the back of the structure housing the forge Eliab built three small rooms. After considerable persuading, he was able to convince Lois and Rebekah to give up their temporary pavilion for the more permanent circumstances of the rooms behind the forge. Eliab would use the reconstructed loft above the work area as his sleeping place. Rebekah insisted that it be made more comfortable. She put in heavy mats that she and he mother wove together. Eliab had never been so comfortable since he was a small boy at home in Jerusalem and Lydda. The thought of Jerusalem and the conditions there caused the old animosities to flare within the young man. He still had a passionate desire to avenge his parents.

Three months after he began working the forge to make implements for farming and utensils for the people in the town two strangers approached Eliab while he was at work. "Are you the smith, the older man inquired?"

Eliab was wary of the men as he guarded his answer. "Yes, what may I do for you?"

"Apparently, you don't recognize your old friends."

Awareness came suddenly. "Justus! I can not believe that it is you! I thought the Romans would have gotten you by now!"

"You are not half as surprised as I am to see you working as a smith. You are hardly the image of a man who is able to do this sort of work."

"I worked for the man whose business this was, but the Roman's killed him because he would not tell where all the young men had gone. When I returned to Dothan months later I took his place."

"You are just the person for whom we have been looking. We need some swords made."

"Justus, I have only enough ingots of iron to make things the villagers and farmers need. There isn't enough for weapons. Besides that, you know full well that the Romans have a ban on the making of any weapons. They will be checking forges throughout the land."

Justus became agitated. "Since when did that matter to you? I thought you wanted to kill Romans!"

"I still do, but I have to think of the people who live around here. They are already hated by the soldiers. If I would be caught making weapons, they would all be punished."

"And what do you think my men and I will do if you refuse to help us?"

Eliab was shocked at Justus' attitude. "You can't mean you would hurt any of these people. That would make you as bad as the Romans!"

"Eliab, we are desperate! Desperation leads us to do what is necessary to keep our cause alive."

Angrily Eliab shot back. "Your cause is for the good of the people, not for your own welfare!"

Rebekah came into the forge with some food for Eliab and overheard that last few exchanges between him and Justus, but pretended to have heard nothing. She set a bowl on a work table and started to leave.

"Now, that my young friend, is something worth fighting for."

Rebekah blushed and then quickly left the work area. Eliab watched as she went outside and around the corner of the structure. It had not occurred to him to think of her as more than a casual friend. He was always too occupied with his own pain and thoughts of fighting back against the invaders of his homeland to consider female companionship as something personal or desirable. Everything was temporary, even his work as a smith. It was a way to live until he could find an opportunity to strike a blow against Rome.

Justus slapped Eliab on the shoulder as he remarked, "You could do us more good as a smith making arms than as a fighter. What do you say?"

Eliab resisted. "I told you, I don't have the extra material to do that. I only have enough to take care of the needs of the community. The last thing I want is to give the Romans and excuse to hurt these people for something I do."

"You have lost your fiery spirit, Eliab. Maybe it is the girl. Maybe, you want to give up the cause and have a family."

Eliab made his argument again and protested that he was still a rebel with a cause, but while he spoke the words the young man knew there was some truth in the evaluation Justus made. Having had it pointed out to him that Rebekah was desirable there grew a hint of interest in her and a feeling that he was missing out on something good. His rebellion had always been more a personal vendetta than a political one, but sometimes it was difficult to separate the two.

"Justus, if you can find some metal ingots and get them to me without anyone knowing it, I will make a few swords but only a few. That will be the end of it."

"What about also taking some of the weapons we have stolen from the Romans and reworking them so that if my men are caught with a sword, they will not know it is one of theirs? If the soldiers recognize their own weaponry, they will execute my men immediately and we will have no chance to make a rescue?"

Eliab thought for a moment and weighed his options. "Maybe a dozen swords, but no more than that. I will have to do it when most people are out of the village. It won't be easy. I know many people here, but there may be some I do not know who might inform on me if they suspect I am helping Zealots. Not everyone agrees with what you are doing. They believe your efforts are making it harder on all the people."

Justus told Eliab he would send a different man each time there was a delivery of swords to be reshaped and each time there would be no more than three weapons wrapped in cloth. It was agreed and the two Zealots made their way out of town. Eliab watched them go and wondered if he should have just refused. His problem was that he had lived and fought along side of those men. He couldn't turn them away without some effort to help the cause.

At supper, Rebekah kept glancing at Eilab. She could tell he was troubled and assumed it was because of the two visitors. He was not eating with the hearty appetite he normally displayed after a long day at the forge. She wanted to ask him about it, but did not want to alert her mother to a problem if none existed. It was after the meal was finished that she asked Eliab to walk with here to the edge of town. He was surprised at the request, but happily agreed.

At first, it was conversation of a general nature and then Rebekah asked, "Did those two men have anything to do with your sour look at supper?"

The two young people stopped walking and faced one another. "Did it show that much? They are men I used to travel with as we made life difficult for Roman encampments. We did hit and run raids. That is why the soldiers have been scouring the country for us and others engaged in the same harassment."

Rebekah frowned deeply as she inquired, "What did your friends want from you?"

"First, I really do not continue to think of them as friends, but I do owe them some respect for taking me in and caring for me after I escaped from Masada. As far as what they wanted; well, that is something I can not talk about!"

Eliab was so emphatic that Rebekah decided not to ask any more questions, but it troubled her heart because she could see that, whatever it was, Eliab was deeply affected by it.

Over the next few months, Eliab and Rebekah became closer than casual friends, but there were no commitments. At the same time as their relationship developed, he was engaged in disguising Roman swords by reworking the metal. The original limit of a dozen became two dozen. Eliab worried that his activities for the Zealots would be discovered and refused to do any more work for Justus and his men. His concern was not for himself but for the people of Dothan if the Romans found out about his participation with the rebels.

As often happens, secrets do not remain secret. A man of the village whose wife had died was interested in Rebekah, even though he was several years older than her. When it became clear that her attentions were focused more in the direction of Eliab, the man passed word that the smith of Dothan might be involved with the enemies of Rome. That was all that was required to bring a squad of soldiers back to the town to see if the rumor had any fact in it.

Eliab was busy at the forge making an implement for one of the locals when his place was entered by three Romans while the others positioned themselves outside. The leader of the squad began to walk around through the shop and picked up various items. He inspected them closely as Eliab stopped what he was doing and watched as the soldier made his way back to the forge.

"So, you are the smith?"

"Yes."

"There was a much older man who was the smith here several months ago when we came through Dothan. You were not here. Why are you here now? Are you not rather light is size to be a smith?"

Eliab lowered his eyes and softly answered the question. "Sir, I am old enough and strong enough. Besides that, the town did not have anyone who knew how to work the forge and metal, so I asked if I could take over this business and the town was happy to have someone who knew a little about being a smith."

"That doesn't really answer my question. Why did you come to Dothan?"

"Sir, I have been without a home since my parents died. I have just been going from one place to another looking for work and a place where I could settle down."

The soldier persisted, "In your many travels, have you become acquainted with groups who have rebelled against the authority of Rome?"

Eliab had no compunction against telling a lie and so he was quick to deny any knowledge of, or association with rebels groups, but he declined to answer a second question of whether he himself had any ill feelings toward Rome. His hesitancy to give an immediate answer brought a sudden response from the officer in charge. He smacked Eliab in the face with an open hand.

"You are too slow to show your loyalty and that leads me to believe you have some sympathy for others who would defy Rome." He turned to his men and ordered a ransacking of the shop. The soldiers from outside joined the others who were turning over all the tables, extinguishing the forge and damaging every thing they could, including breaking the handles from the hammers.

"We will be back when you are not expecting us, so you had better learn quickly where your loyalties are, and it better be your Roman masters!"

With that warning, the soldiers left Dothan. They also left a very angry young man. If there was any thought of rejecting rebellion as an answer to Israel's woes, those thoughts had been destroyed by the behavior of the soldiers.

Rebekah and Lois waited for the Romans to leave and then came into the destroyed shop to check on Eliab. They could immediately see how angry he was. He picked up what was left of one of his hammers and began to repeatedly slam it against the anvil until he had no more strength to swing the heavy tool.

Lois put her arms around Eliab to consol him. "Son, what has happened to upset you so and why did the soldiers trash this place?"

Eliab slumped to the dirt floor with his back against a post. "They suspect me. They think I have aided the rebels, but could find no evidence. The officer struck me and ordered the others to wreck everything in sight. He warned that they will come back."

"But, my boy, if you have done nothing wrong, why would they want to come back again?"

"I think someone knew I was fashioning swords for the men I used to be with and sent word to the Romans. My guess is that it was Salah, the rug maker. I have noticed how he has looked at Rebekah ever since his wife died. He thinks I am his rival."

Lois questioned, "And are you?"

"I very well could be if your daughter gave me some encouragement." Rebekah turned away and walked out of the shop. "See, even now she turns from me!"

"Eliab, there is just one thing that prevents my daughter from showing her affection for you, besides your association with Zealots."

"And what is that?"

"She is a follower of the Messiah and you have been critical of any belief that Jesus of Nazareth is the one of whom the prophets spoke. Two people who are separated by truth cannot live together in harmony. The prophet Amos wrote 'Can two walk together except they be in agreement?' That is a truth that cannot be violated or there can be no happiness."

The young man turned his head away from Lois. "This has been the story of my life! My father and grandfather could not agree because they each had strong views about the Nazarene and it divided our family. I was always pulled back and forth between them, but I settled for my grandfather's view because he was a priest. He should have known the truth!"

Lois assisted Eliab to his feet and led him into the rooms behind the shop. She prepared some broth and had the young man sit at the table. She sat opposite him while Rebekah remained outside. "You said that your grandfather should have known the truth and you are correct, he should have, but it was your father who searched the scriptures for the truth and he found it. Truth is not someone's opinion. Truth can be verified by actual evidence. Did you ever hear your grandfather quote from the scrolls of the prophets?"

"No. He quoted from Deuteronomy and Leviticus. He spoke often of the laws and the traditions. When my father tried to show him passages from the prophets, he would not listen. He felt my father was blaspheming because he spoke of Jesus as the Messiah."

"And, Eliab, what do you believe?"

"I believe you and Rebekah and the other follower of Jesus are sincere, but I just cannot bring myself to believe that the Messiah would come and then allow himself to be put to death! It makes no sense!"

"Yes, it makes no sense, unless you understand why he came and why he died. I heard him say with my own ears that he, the Messiah, must suffer many things. He had to be rejected by the elders of our people, along with the chief priest and scribes, and that in the end he would be killed and then rise from the dead on the third day. He said whoever was ashamed of him when he returns in great glory the Father would be ashamed of that person. I am not ashamed of my Jesus and I know in my own heart that he has the power to forgive sins and change lives. He changed mine. "

Eliab angrily stood to his feet. "No! Do not start telling me about him dying! The real Messiah would fight back! I cannot give my allegiance to a coward! The true Messiah would not submit to what was done to him! He would be like a Zealot!"

"Son, you did not hear me. He is alive and his Spirit resides in believers and leads us in paths of righteousness for his name's sake. You are too upset to let your mind be open to the truth. Jesus was no coward.

He stood face to face with the Scribes and Pharisees and told them what they were; blind guides and hypocrites. It was telling the truth that got him killed, but it was also love that kept him on the cross. He loved us so much he was willing to pay the penalty of our sins to satisfy the justice of God."

Eliab interrupted: "Justice! I see no justice in that and I see no justice in all of Israel! Where is God that he would allow this to come upon the people? Where is justice for my parents and my grandfather? And what about justice for me? I have found a woman I could love and begin to have a life with, but Jesus stands between us!"

"Son, when two people agree together there is peace."

Eliab turned to leave. "I thank you for your many kindnesses to me and for giving me the nearest thing to a home I have known for many years, but I cannot stay here while the killers of my family are occupying our land. I will find my own justice!"

Lois followed Eliab to the door to urge him to stay. "There is nothing good to be found in seeking retribution. Killing Romans will not bring your parents back. I too have lost family, but the Messiah has given me peace of mind and a hope for the future with him in paradise."

Eliab turned and faced Lois. "You have been like a mother to me, but what you say makes no sense. You say the Nazarene is still alive, but that goes against reason."

"Eliab, he is alive. He arose from the tomb and ascended to his throne in heaven, but he also lives in my heart. He guides me every day and helps me cope with a world that is at war with Jehovah. If you would only give up this quest for revenge and turn your life over to the Savior, you would find peace. You and Rebekah might then find a life together, but it will not happen until you are right in your spirit."

"If only what you say is true, but I am not ready to accept the Nazarene as my Messiah. Please Lois, please tell Rebekah goodbye for me."

"No, Eliab. That is something you must do yourself. She waits by the well where you met when you first came to Dothan."

It was not something Eliab wanted to do, but he could not leave without seeing Rebekah one more time. He would always regret it if he left and said nothing to her, even though he did not want to face the disappointment he would see in her large brown eyes.

She was facing the well as Eliab approached and did not turn around when she heard his footsteps stop behind her. "You are leaving."

"Yes, but how did you know?"

"It was the slow way you came to me. If you had good news for me, you would have walked faster. I have sensed your restlessness for several days. You cannot hide your emotions. They reveal themselves in the way you walk and talk, and in everything you do."

Eliab was torn between his deep feelings for Rebekah and his passionate commitment to gain some personal satisfaction by releasing his hatred of the Romans upon any he might encounter in his wandering. "I don't really want to leave, but I have to go and it is not safe for you and the others if I stay here."

"Eliab, that is thoughtful of you, but there is a greater reason why you want to leave, is there not? Your heart is for war, not peace. As long as this is true, anyone who comes too close to you will not find peacefulness. Jesus said that a double minded man is unstable in all his ways."

The young man replied, "You and your mother are very discerning people. In so many words, she told me the same thing. She says your Messiah can give peace, but I guess I am not ready to believe it. I am so very sorry. I have a great fondness for you and I think we could have a good life together. It is just this ache in my heart to avenge my parents. It will not let go of me! I don't know if anything can take it away."

"Not even the love of Jehovah?"

"Not even his love, nor yours: not yet."

CHAPTER EIGHT

Alive at Last

The sun had climbed half way toward noon as Eliab left the edge of Dothan on his way south. After a mile he stopped. Was this the direction he wanted to go? His departure was so impulsive that he had not taken the time to calculate what he was going to do next. He sat down on a large rock and began to consider whether he should go on south to the area of Jerusalem, but quickly rejected that notion. There was nothing left for him in upper Judea and he had no interest at all in returning to the desert bordering the Dead Sea. There was nothing for him there either. The Roman garrisons in the north were also to be avoided.

Wherever Eliab chose to go, it had to be someplace suitable for earning a living. He had enough of trying to be a smith. The Romans were too interested in anyone in that trade. He had saved enough coins in his travel pouch that he could survive several days as along as he was very frugal and did not eat very much. That fact triggered the idea that perhaps he should leave Israel and try to find a place much farther north.

Eliab had heard his father speak of places like Cilicia and Phrygia. Perhaps he could find a new life among the Gentiles, after all, he had a Gentile last name, but would that be running away from his sworn pledge to kill Roman soldiers? Eliab reasoned that there were Roman soldiers everywhere and so what did it matter which ones would pay for the deaths of his loved ones?

To avoid hiking north over the rough mountains, Eliab headed west to Caesarea located right on the coast. It was dusk when he arrived at the edge of the town. Not wanting to sleep on the ground for fear of scorpions and other creatures, the young man quietly made his way up to the flat roof of a house and lay down with his head on his outer garment which he had rolled up for a pillow. Exhaustion quickly induced a deep sleep that lasted until the rays of the rising sun in the east broke over the mountains and began to bathe the coastal plain with its warmth.

Eliab was startled to his senses by the brightness of the light. He had expected to awaken early enough that he could have gotten down from the roof before people were beginning to become active. As he lifted his head to check the area surrounding the house, someone saw him.

"What are you doing up there? Come down this minute and be ready with a good answer!" The voice barking the orders was that of a man with very long white hair and beard. He had a walking stick in his right hand and waved it toward Eliab as he spoke. "Come on! Do not be so slow about it!"

"Please forgive me, sir. I arrived so late last night I had no place to lay my head and did not think sleeping on this roof was a wrong thing to do."

"What is your name?"

"My name is Marcus."

"Marcus what?"

"Just plain Marcus, sir."

"What happened: did your parents have so many children they ran out of names?"

Eliab decided that what the old man said was a statement and not a question, so he chose to keep silent. When he reached the ground the man poked him in the chest with the end of the stick. It was not a hard poke. It seemed more to test Eliab's reaction.

"You do not intimidate easily, do you?"

Again, Eliab gave no reply. The two men just stood and looked at each other for a few moments and then the old man spoke. "Are you hungry? Have you had anything to eat for the last few days?"

The young man reluctantly replied, "A little. I have some bread and I was going to buy some cheese in the town."

"Buy it, or steal it?"

"I only steal if I have nothing left with which to buy."

The old man burst out laughing. "An honest thief! That is wonderful! You have made my day, young man. My house is over there. Come with me and eat my bread and cheese. It is free to an honest thief."

Since the man with the walking stick seemed harmless enough, Eliab followed as the slightly stooped, whitehead elderly one stabbed the ground with the cane to help him keep his balance. Inside the small structure that was more a hut than a house, there were two small rooms: one for sleeping and the other for everything else. There was a small short-legged table which made chairs unnecessary, so Eliab sat on a mat spread out on the earthen floor.

"Could you tell me what I should call you, sir?"

"My parents named me Reuel."

"Just Reuel.? Did they run out of names?"

"You are too quick with a disrespectful remark, Marcus. Or should I call you Marcus Marcus? I know that is not your family name. If it were, I would not have invited you to my house?"

"How do you know I am not a Gentile?"

"You don't look like a Gentile. I am a Jew and I would not allow a Gentile in my house, so how did you get that name?"

"Well, Reuel, my father worked for a Gentile merchant and before the man died he adopted him and gave him the name I told you."

The old man brought the bread and cheese to the table and slowly sank down on his mat. "So what is a rich Jewish boy doing sleeping on borrowed roofs?"

"My first name is Eliab and I am not rich. The Romans took care of that. They also killed my family."

Reuel munched on a piece of bread at the same time he spoke. "So you are alone in this world. So am I, but if I was as young as you and had suffered the injustice of the Romans as you have, I would be angry and wanting to fight."

"I am and I have done that. I still plan to do more when I find a way to support myself!" The bread and cheese were very dry and Eliab nearly choked on his words. "Sir, do you have a little wine?"

"I have no wine, but I do have some tepid water."

"You have no table wine?"

"Eliab, I am a Nazirite. As a young man, I took a vow not to drink wine, nor cut my hair as a sign that I have dedicated myself to Jehovah to be pure for him."

"Sounds pretty boring to me."

"I admit there are certain issues, but that would not stop me from eliminating as many of Jehovah's enemies as I could if I were able."

Eliab continued his verbal jousting with the old man. "So, you would be another Samson!"

"Do not make fun of the vow or those who take it."

"I was not; honestly."

"Eat your food and then go slay some Romans for me!"

"Reuel, you are a contradiction: a holy man with the thirst for blood. Just as I said, you remind me of what I have heard about Samson."

Reuel snarled, "Philistines or Romans; they are all the same to me."

Eliab finished his morsel of bread and thanked his benefactor. He took his leave of the old man and began walking north to Dor where he saw a small contingent of soldiers. He remembered to keep his eyes looking down and not look at the faces of the men. Eye contact might have invited a response from one or more of the rough looking warriors. By late afternoon Eliab was well beyond Dor and had reached the mouth of the Kishon River where he decided to rest and soak his hot and hurting feet it the water.

Moments after Eliab sat down and removed his sandals, he was joined by another traveler. He was tall, thin, and clean shaven. "Do you mind if I sit here? I have not had the opportunity to speak with another soul all day."

Eliab answered, "I have no objection. I could use some companionship to break up the boredom of my journey."

The young man, who appeared to be a few years junior in age to

Eliab, took a seat but did not rest his feet in the water. "Could you tell me your name? Mine is Onan."

"Eliab. My name is Eliab."

"I have heard that name somewhere in the past. I believe I will remember where and when if I think hard enough. Were you on Masada?"

Eliab chose not to answer the question. Instead, he asked, "Were you? I heard that that everyone was killed."

Onan replied, "Not everyone. My mother and four other children besides me hid in a cave and were captured. Mother died weeks later as we were being marched north and west to Joppa on the coast. They were going to send us with several others on a ship to Rome to be slaves. I managed to slip away the night after my mother died and have been without a home since then."

"We have much in common, especially a hatred for the Romans."

Onan persisted, "I still think I know your name. You were there! Yes, you were on Masada! I remember you leading the younger children in songs while the parents prepared for the assault against us. What have you been doing since then?"

"Sometimes killing Romans and sometimes hiding from them. I am on my way now to regions far to the north where I may find more to feel my wrath."

"Are there not enough in Israel for you?"

"Too many! I need to find more men who will join with me to resist the enemy. I have lost contact with my former companions."

Eliab and Onan made an oath to seek out others who feel as they do and begin to make life as difficult for the soldiers of the empire as they had opportunity. Their next stop was Ptolemais. It was dangerous for the young men to show themselves during the daylight and so they elected to sneak into an animal shed in the countryside south of the town. Hunger was the biggest problem. The only food available was wild berries and stolen fruit from an orchard. What they needed was some meat.

There was a long uninhabited stretch of land between Ptolemais and Tyre. They would find no meat along the coast, except fish, but neither of them knew anything about salt water fishing, nor what to use to try to make a catch. Their best opportunity was to go inland a few miles and look for a stray sheep or goat they could steal. Unfortunately there were none to be found.

As the two vagabonds traveled farther north and a few miles in from the coast to avoid the city of Tyre, Eliab and Onan came upon three men a few years older than Eliab. They were sitting around a small fire and eating some kind of meat. The moment the men heard someone approaching, they got to their feet and placed there hands on weapons.

Eliab spoke first, "Please, we mean no trouble. We are weary travelers and very hungry. Could you be so kind as to share a bite of your food with us? If we were able, we would pay." He was not going to indicate to them, or to Onan, that he had money. He feared he might become a victim.

One of the strangers asked, "Where are you two going?"

Onan replied, "North."

One of the men snapped back, "North takes in a lot of territory!"

Eliab wanted to keep their true plans to themselves. There was no way to know if these people were sympathetic to the Romans or to the rebels and he did not want to ask. "We hope to find work somewhere between here and the cities along the coast of Cilicia and Pamphylia."

"Best of luck to you! The way the Romans have been cracking down on Jews of fighting age, we are all fortunate not to have been swept up in their clutches and shipped off to some other country as slaves."

Eliab was happy to hear the comment that indicated they were in safe company. He asked, "Where were your homes?"

The heavy set man, who seemed to be the oldest, spoke for the others. We are all from Judea: Hebron to be exact. After the fall of Jerusalem no place in the area was safe and we have been slowly going north also, but it would not look good for so many men to be traveling together. In the morning we must go our separate ways. We have considered turning eastward to Damascus. It is rumored that it is a friendlier region. Perhaps we will find employment there."

Eliab agreed that they should not travel together and the group settled down for the night. He tried to sleep, but his mind kept entertaining the idea of by passing Asia altogether. He had heard that Asia was a rather dangerous place for strangers. Greece might be a better choice and the best way to get there would be by a ship. There was a port at Sidon where he could find passage. Eliab would have to separate from Onan since he did not have enough money to purchase passage for both of them.

When he informed Onan the next morning that his plans had changed and his intentions were to find a way to get to Greece, Onan was disappointed, but decided to throw in his lot with the other men, if they would have him, and travel east. He had no desire to go into Greek territory.

At first light, Eliab left the group to go to the coast and the town of Sidon which faced the Mediterranean Sea. It was a city which the Romans gave the right of self-government. As a place of cultural development and one impacted by the followers of Christ, there was a measure of freedom which set Eliab at ease. His fear of discovery faded while he waited for a ship to take him to the north and west.

After some difficult bartering with a ship's captain, Eliab was able to book passage as a laborer to load and unload cargo at every port of call between Sidon and Neapolis, the port city serving Philippi. He had no plans beyond that, but getting to Neapolis through the waters of the Aegean Sea would be quite an adventure. Many ships that attempted the voyage found the sudden storms and contrary winds not survivable.

To avoid the unfavorable winds of the open sea, Captain Heirodoplus sailed close to the Phoenician and Syrian coast and then westward under the coast of Cilicia and Pamphylia to the first port of call at Myra. The city was located two miles from the sea on a navigable river. It was an important stopping place for grain ships sailing out of Egypt. While participating in the unloading of cargo, a shifting load fell against Eliab pinning him between the cargo and the dock. The result of the accident was he suffered a broken right leg.

Captain Heirodoplus had no choice but to leave Eliab at Myra. Two seamen carried him to a guest house near the docks where a traveling physician who was temporarily housed in the same place attended to Eliab. The man seemed to be associated with spreading a message of a teacher they spoke of as the Anointed One. This physician expertly attended to setting Eliab's broken bone.

Soon after Eliab Marcus began to feel better he was introduced to the leader of the small band of travelers which included the physician. One man in the group was named Paulus. It was soon learned that he was a former Pharisee who had become a follower of Jesus whom he claimed he had met after Jesus was resurrected from the dead. Paulus and his companions were waiting at Myra to book passage on a ship that was going to the west to supply Rome with much needed grain for food.

Paulus began to witness of how the Anointed One, Jesus, was God's Son and could provide forgiveness of sin and grace to live a life pleasing to Jehovah. After a few more days in which Paulus spoke with Eliab and offered prayer for the young man, Eliab admitted to Paulus that he was almost persuaded to become a disciple of Jesus, but there was too much hatred stored in the man's mind that gripped him tightly and so he continued to resist believing the truth Paulus proclaimed.

The hardness of Eliab's heart remained after Paulus and Loukas, the physician, had to bid him goodbye and board the ship for which they had been waiting. It was then that Eliab learned that the man who had been counseling him concerning the way of salvation was on his way to Rome under guard to be tried as an enemy of the Roman Empire.

With his funds nearly exhausted from the long delay while his leg healed, Eliab finally gained passage from Myra on a ship going through the many islands between the coast of Asia and the open sea. The First stop was Miletus on the south shore of the Latonian Gulf. The series of small islands dotting the waters west of the Asian coast included Cos, Samos, and Patmos.

The Romans had turned Patmos into a prison island and a number of the followers of Christ were held there and forced to do hard labor. Some of the prisoners were members of the Christian church at Ephesus, the capitol city of the province of Lydia. As the ship began to leave port from Miletus the winds steadily increased and whipped the waves into giant frothy battering rams that pounded the sides of the vessel and swamped the decks, driving the ship toward the rocky west side of Samos.

Every effort was made to lighten the load by casting cargo into the sea, but it was to no avail. The wind and waves repeatedly bashed the ship against the rocks. A huge gaping hole in the middle section of the starboard side began taking on water rapidly and the captain ordered everyone to abandon the ship and try to swim to Samos.

In addition to the crew and a few passengers like Eliab, there were six Roman soldiers charged with protecting part of the cargo destined as supplies for a garrison in northern Greece. They and the captain were the last ones to leave the sinking vessel. Eliab had jumped into the water and secured a floating piece of wood just before the soldiers shed the heavy pieces of their uniforms and plunged into the raging caldron.

One of the soldiers came along side of Eliab and began tugging at his piece of shattered wood planking. There was no intention of sharing the life saving flotsam with Eliab and a struggle began for its possession. Considering Eliab's hatred for all Roman soldiers, he was not about to allow his enemy to take away his only means of safety. While clinging desperately to the board with his left hand and arm the soldier struck Eliab a hard blow against his jaw with his right fist, but the young Jew would not release his hold. At that same instant, a huge wave washed over both of the men. Eliab emerged from the wave still firmly hanging onto the board, but the soldier was nowhere to be found.

Either the undertow had pulled him back into deeper water or he was rendered unconscious against the rocks just beneath the waves. In either case, Eliab's wrestling for his own survival and the disappearance of the Roman soldier was observed and when he finally was able to drag himself up onto the rocks where the waves could not wash him back into the sea, he was seized by two of the soldiers who had already gained the rocks.

"You will hang for what you did out there! You murdered a soldier of the empire!"

"No! Not so! He was trying to kill me! I did not take his life! It was the sea!"

"There is no defense for anyone who takes the life of a Roman! As soon as we are able, we will take you to Ephesus to be beaten and then crucified."

"I cannot be crucified! I am a Roman citizen and you know the law. If I am judged by Roman law to be guilty, I must die by the sword."

"You look like a Jew to us. How can you also be a Roman?"

"By adoption, with all the rights of a Roman citizen. My father was given the name Markus and adopted by a wealthy Roman. I have inherited my citizenship!"

"We will let the court decide your fate, but I can tell you right now. You will be found guilty."

"Then I will appeal all the way to Rome if I have to."

"Appeal all you want, Jew! If I have anything to do with it, you will never get to Rome!"

When the seas calmed down Eliab was escorted in a small craft from Samos to the port of Ephesus and placed in a rat infested prison to wait for his day in court. That day did not come for six months. Had it not been for the good physical condition Eliab enjoyed prior to his capture, he probably would have died before his case was heard, as was the fate of many prisoners.

The winter months were the worst because of the cold and dampness in the cell blocks. Clothing was whatever a man had on him when he was imprisoned. The food was slop, unless someone had friends on the outside who could bribe a guard. Eliab had no one to bring him assistance. There was always a great deal of coughing and sounds of lung disease among the inmates.

One morning in January, the iron cell door clanged open and four soldiers marched over to Eliab and jerked him to his feet. The shackles were removed and an iron collar with a chain attached was placed around his neck.

"You have an appointment with a judge, Jew! At long last you will get what is coming to you."

With those spiteful words hurled at him, Eliab was marched out into the sunlight and down a short cobblestone street to a large structure that was obviously some official building considering that it was distinctly Roman in architecture. When the soldiers shoved him into a large room with a robed man sitting on an elevated platform, it truly became real to Eliab that he was to be judged.

"The prisoners name?" demanded the robed person.

"Your Majesty, his name is Eliab Marcus."

"A Jewish first name and a Roman last name? How did you come by this name? Speak up!"

"I inherited both names."

The lead soldier smacked Eliab in the face. "Address your judge with respect! Call him 'Your Majesty!'"

Eliab recovered from the blow and used the proper response and then rehearsed how he had come by a Roman name and with it Roman citizenship.

"What are the charges against this man?"

"Murder, Your Majesty."

"Who did he kill?"

"A Roman soldier, Your Majesty."

The magistrate look down at the prisoner and demanded, "And what have you to say for yourself before I pass sentence?"

"Your Majesty, I and six soldiers were abroad a ship that sank in a storm and we were all fighting the waves to save our lives. A soldier and I were clinging to the same driftwood when a huge wave broke over us and the soldier never surfaced. For this reason, and this reason only, I have been falsely charged and thrown in prison these many months. I have had little in the way of food or the treatment due a Roman citizen."

"Who witnessed this loss of the soldier's life?"

No one spoke up and so Eliab gave his answer. "Your Majesty, I believe no one did besides me. Everyone else was trying to save themselves from the deep."

"Then you deny the truth of the charges?"

"I do! Your Majesty."

The judge considered what he should do for several minutes while everyone in the room waited in silence. Finally, he was ready to give his decision. "It is the word of a Jew passing as a Roman citizen against the written report of soldiers of the empire. And, on that basis, I sentence you to death by the sword."

Eliab struggled against the strong arms that held him and cried out, "As a Roman citizen I appeal to Ceasar! Is not Rome governed by laws and those laws provide citizens the right of appeal? Will you deal justly according to your own laws?"

The judge was caught in a difficult position. He was bound by strict rules and procedures. Although he wished to have done with Eliab, he could not violate the very laws that governed the empire.

"Put this man back in the prison until I decide to what jurisdiction he shall be sent."

"Your Majesty, am I not also entitled to be kept in a prison separate from those pitiful creatures who have no standing under Roman citizenship?"

By this time, the judge was becoming exasperated, but because he did not wish to be seen by a superior court as having mistreated a citizen, he had Eliab transferred to another part of the prison. Whereas the conditions were somewhat better, it was still a prison. It was there that Eliab languished for another year before he was given a hearing by another judge who agreed with the former sentence, but commuted it to life at hard labor.

The day following the sentence, Eliab, still in chains, was placed aboard a small ship with other prisoners and sent to Patmos, a tiny wind swept island twenty-eight miles south of Samos. It was merely ten miles long and six miles wide at the broadest location. Patmos had an irregular coastline and was composed of a terrain made of volcanic rock and was nearly treeless. The several hills rose as high as eight hundred feet above the surrounding sea. The harbor of the island was Scala; the chief city.

Eliab was sentenced to live and die on that rock. At nearly thirty-six years of age, he still held tightly to his hatred for all things Roman and his hate grew and ate at his soul as he saw the small island being approached by the ship that bore him to his fate. This was not how he expected to die. In Eliab's mind, he would go down in battle. The despair that swept over him brought thoughts of suicide. That impulse quickly passed. Somehow and in some manner, he was determined to escape Patmos and continue his search for a satisfactory retribution against the Romans. He now had another reason to hate them.

With the rising and falling from the wave action and the straining of the vessel against the mooring hawsers, it was difficult for people to leave the ship. As the prisoners disembarked and were being herded to various places to work out their punishment, Eliab was taken to a location above Scala where there were a number of caves or grottos. For twelve hours a day he was destined to break large rocks into small ones. Twice during those hours he was allowed a very brief period of rest and to eat the horrible soup provided to the prisoners and also to take care of other necessities. The timing of this break from labor was at the choosing of the guards who hated their assigned duty and often took out their displeasure on the exiles. A lashing across the back of a prisoner who seemed to be lagging in performing his work reinforced the obvious: the guards were the masters.

As Eliab attended to his hammering of the rocks over the next few months, he noticed that a delegation of two to three visitors were allowed to bring items to a very old man who lived in a cave near where Eliab was posted. The old man was past being able to break rocks and he did not seem to be a prisoner in the common sense of the word.

Without drawing too much attention to himself, Eliab began to break rocks closer to the cave where he could observe more clearly what was happening when the visitors came to see the old man. They brought him small amounts of food and pieces of parchment. He in turn gave them rolled up pieces of parchment upon which there was writing.

It seemed to Eliab that this old, white-haired man had certain privileges, but they did not make his situation any more comfortable than others who were no longer able to do manual labor. As Eliab Marcus observed the ancient one, he saw him dictating to another person what was to be written on the parchment. When he grew tired, the old one rested and then the dictating resumed.

After a few months on the rock, the person acting as a scribe became ill and a search was made for someone to temporarily take his place. Since Eliab appeared to be better educated and more articulate than many of the prisoners, he was interviewed as to his qualifications to be a scribe. Eliab revealed that he was the grandson of a high ranking Jewish priest and educated by both the priest and his own father who had been a businessman. With that information in hand the overseer of the island prison took him to meet with a man by the name of John. The overseer described John to Eliab as a devout follower of Jesus, the crucified one, and that John was one of the original followers of Jesus.

Eliab replied, "I know of him. My father met John and others of the disciples, some of whom were called Apostles."

The officer said, "You should make that known to the ancient one, or he may not want to use you in his service."

Eliab was led into the grotto and presented to John who steadily gazed upon the ragged looking prisoner. "How well do you write, my son?"

"Very well, sir."

"You need not call me sir. I am a prisoner like you. Sit here next to me and let me see you write your name, your father's name, and where you were born."

Eliab took the quill and ink, along with a small scrap of parchment and did as he was told. "Here is my sample."

John took the sample and read the names and place of birth. "You were born in Jerusalem. How old were you when Jerusalem was destroyed?"

"I was almost eleven years of age."

"You survived the onslaught obviously, but what of your family?"

"All died."

"I see that your father's name was Andrew Marcus. That seems familiar to me, but it was so long ago."

"My father became of follower of your Jesus. He met him in Galilee after the reported resurrection of the Nazarene."

John had a curious look come over his face. He thought about what Eliab had just said. "I noticed that you referred to the Master as 'your Jesus' indicating that you are not one of his followers, but you say that your father was. You also spoke of the Master as the Nazarene. So, it would seem that you have not become a believer."

Eliab responded. "The Master, as you call him, is not my enemy, I'm just not ready to accept him as the Messiah for whom my people have waited so long."

John placed the sample of Eliab's writing on a small, crude table beside him and addressed the man. "May I please enlighten you about something? You cannot be neutral about the Master. Either he becomes your brother and friend: your own Savior, or you are a soul who is lost and shut out from the Kingdom of God. Secondly, I am just as much a Jew as you are. Your people are also my people."

With a bit of impertinence Eliab asked, "Are you as much a Jew as my grandfather Abdi who was a priest?"

"Indeed, young man, I am. Being a disciple of Jesus the Messiah does not make me less a Jew than you are, or your grandfather was."

"Old man, your words make me exceedingly curious, especially since you and my father once met and you have first hand knowledge of what Jesus taught. May I be your scribe until your assistant is able to resume his work?"

"You may, but only if you are born again."

Eliab appeared to be slightly irritated at John's words. "I have heard my father speak of being born anew and it made no sense to me then and none now."

"Young man, there is a physical birth and there is a spiritual birth. Merely being born physically, regardless of one's heritage and good manners, does not prepare a person for to enter God's heaven. In the words of the Master, 'That which is born of flesh is flesh and that which is born of the Spirit is Spirit.' Furthermore, flesh and blood cannot inherit the Kingdom, therefore everyone who would make his eternal abode with God must be made alive spiritually."

"I don't understand. How can that happen?

"The Spirit of God must come into your life and the Messiah must be your Lord. Until this happens, a person cannot become part of God's Kingdom. You must be born of water and the Spirit.

"I have heard of baptism by water. Is that required? Where on this rock would there be enough water to be immersed?"

John fixed his gaze upon the man and could see his confusion. "When Jesus said that a person must be born of water and the Spirit, it was not water baptism of which he spoke. The phrase 'water and the Spirit' is a common Hebrew device to express something with emphasis.

The same thing is repeated, but in slightly different words meaning the same thing. What I am telling you is that God's Spirit must come into you. This happens as you are being saved from your sin and unbelief. The Holy Spirit seals you into the family of God by His grace through faith."

Eliab protested, "But what if I have kept all of the laws of Moses and all of the rituals of our people? After all, I am a descendant of Abraham. Does this not make me acceptable to God? I am a Jew and the son and grandson of Jews."

John again looked closely into the face of Eliab. "I will ask you one thing, young man: have you kept all of the laws of Moses perfectly and observed each and every festival and ritual?"

"No, of course not! No one can do that."

"Then by your own admission, you have missed the mark of perfection. It is called sin. When the first two human beings failed to live perfectly it was called sin and through Adam the disease of sin has passed down to the whole human race. God told Adam that if he disobeyed His will, Adam would die and death you pass upon us all."

Eliab was perplexed. "Who then can be saved from God's judgment?"

"Jesus said, 'he who believes in me shall never die.' The Master was speaking of the everlasting death that follows this life. He also, declared, 'I am the way, the truth, and the life, no one comes unto the Father except by me.'"

Eliab stood to his feet and walked away for a brief moment and then returned to John. "I met a man named Paulus years ago who spoke to me about faith in the Messiah and I strongly resisted what he said to me. I hear your words and what you say Jesus said and I am still finding it hard to accept all of this as being true."

"Eliab, you must pray to God and ask him to open your heart and mind. Sins must be confessed and forgiveness sought. Neither you nor I know how long we have to breathe the air of physical life and if you wish to escape the condemnation of eternal death and know that all your sin has been wiped away so that when this life is done you can stand before God as his own dear child, you must do it soon. You have seen much death; this I can tell. Now I ask you to embrace everlasting life by receiving the Messiah as you own Lord and Master."

"Ancient one, I am struggling with this idea of repenting of my sins, for I have pledged to commit more sin to avenge the death of my parents at the hands of the Romans. It is hard to say I repent of that and of the Romans I have already killed. I know nothing of how such a thing can be forgiven, by me or by God."

John placed a hand on Eliab's shoulder, "Nevertheless, you must be forgiven to receive spiritual life. With God's Spirit you will be able to forgive others. To forgive is to give up the right to be angry against another and give up the right to get even. Jesus forgives us our sins when we repent. He gives up his right as God to punish us."

Eliab shook his head. He was struggling with all that he had heard. "My father told me how he heard Jesus ask God in heaven to forgive those who crucified him. I will spend the night in prayer. It would be wonderful to know such mercy."

Darkness fell across the landscape and all work had ceased. Without light for most of the prisoners, they each retired to their own piece of ground and found what covering they could against the cold night air. Eliab was invited by John to share a corner of the cave, but he did not sleep. He tried to pray as he promised he would, but it was a strange exercise and the words would not come to him. He thought of all he had been told concerning Jesus by his father, by Rebekah and her mother, by Paulus, and now John. They were all so sincere, but Abdi's strong denunciation of Jesus as being the Messiah mingled with the claims of the others and only added confusion.

When morning came and Eliab approached John, he found the Apostle in prayer and so he waited until it was appropriate to ask questions. What could he say? Surely John would be expecting him to declare his faith in the Messiah, but he wasn't ready for that. There were gaps he wanted filled in before he would make a commitment.

John knew Eliab was standing nearby and eventually concluded his praying to attend to the man who wanted to be his scribe. "Have you decided to follow Jesus as your Lord and Savior? Have you found forgiveness in your heart for those who have wronged you?"

"How can I forgive those who killed my parents?"

"Eliab, forgiveness means you must leg go of the anger that has captured you and has made you more of a prisoner than Rome has."

"That is too hard for me!"

"It is not too hard for God. He will forgive you and he will help you forgive others."

"I beg your pardon, John, but I have more questions. There has to be some good thing I must do in order to earn God's favor to grant me access to his heaven. What would it be? What work may I perform?"

"I will tell you what the Master told Nicodemus."

"Nicodemus? My father spoke with him about his association with Jesus."

"Did your father tell you what Jesus said?"

"If he did, I don't remember."

"Nicodemus asked a question similar to yours and Jesus said that God loved mankind so much that he gave his only begotten son that when a person believes in him, that person will have everlasting life. Did you hear the word, 'gave'? Being rescued from one's sin and eternal damnation is a gift from God to those who believe in his Messiah as the Savior of the world. That means both Jews and Gentiles."

Eliab was astonished. "Salvation is a gift? You mean I can't earn God's favor?"

John assured the startled young man, "That is exactly what Jesus said. The Apostle named Paulus, whom you met before your journey to this place, said it another way in his inspired writings: 'The wages of sin is death, but the gift of God is eternal life in Messiah Jesus our Lord.' It is called grace. That means God will forgive you of your sin and make you his own eternal child even though you don't deserve the blessing."

"There must be something I can do!"

"The only thing you can do is to open your heart to God's love and the gift of his Son. Let go of your pride, your trust in traditions, and your stubbornness. Trust God for a new life."

"If I do this: if I pray for salvation, will it get me off this island and free from the Romans?"

"We don't bargain with God. If He chooses to have us die here, or if He let's us go back to the mainland as free men, that is His choice. This I do know, unless you call on Him without reservations and deal making, you will probably die on this rock and, for certain, you will spend eternity in outer darkness where there is weeping and wailing and gnashing of teeth. Eliab Marcus, make you choice while you are able!"

A strange and powerful presence took hold of Eliab and he suddenly fell to his knees as he cried out to God to forgive him of his hatred and his evil deeds of which there were many. He asked that God's Spirit would take control of his life. Moments later, while still on his knees, he looked up to John. "I do believe in Jesus as my Savior and Lord. I understand things that before made no sense to me. A great burden has been lifted from me and I feel free, even though I am still a prisoner of Rome."

"Marcus, you have finally come to know what I have known. Though my body is in bondage, my soul belongs to God and my person is free."

CHAPTER NINE

Salt Slave

For the next several weeks following Eliab Marcus' conversion to faith in Jesus as his Messiah and Savior, he served the Apostle John by transcribing letters to a number of associates in the Christian ministry. On the day Eliab was to begin writing John's dictation of messages for seven churches in Asia which the risen Lord had given the Apostle, a centurion entered the grotto and informed him that he was being transferred to serve out his sentence in Europe.

"You will become closely acquainted with salt over the rest of your miserable life. The privileges you have enjoyed the past few months will not be known where you are going."

John struggled to his feet and embraced Eliab. "My brother, God will be with you wherever you go. Keep the faith! Walk worthy of our Lord and anticipate that glorious day when we will all be with him in the heavenly Father's house."

Eliab stifled his emotions as he momentarily held on to the ancient Apostle. "Thank you for opening my eyes to the truth and helping me understand how all the things that have happened to me since I was a child have been worked together to bring me to the Messiah. I will cherish these several weeks in your presence."

"Give God the glory, my brother! Give him all the glory!" was John's advise to Eliab. "Always give God the glory."

The Roman officer interrupted, "This is enough! Take the prisoner and follow me!" The centurion had held his anger as long as he could and ordered Eliab shackled and led away to Scala and the port where he was placed on board a ship. The destination was the coast of northeast Italia.

Sailing around the tip of Achaia at the present season of the year was a very dangerous journey. To avoid a potential disaster, ships were taken out of the water at Corinth, unloaded and moved across the land bridge between the Aegean Sea and the waters leading to the Adriatic Sea.

When the task of rolling the vessel over the isthmus on logs and launched again was completed, Eliab, other prisoners, and all the cargo was made ready to began its journey north along the coast of Dalmatia. At a series of fingers of land, some of which reached twenty-five miles out into the Adriatic and others formed barrier Islands along the coast, the ship encountered a sudden squall that pushed the vessel against rocks and the rudder was broken. Without the ability to steer away from the shoals the ship began to break up. For the second time Eliab found himself the victim of a sinking ship.

Quartus, the centurion, did not want to release the prisoners from their shackles, but he also feared his pagan gods' retribution if he did nothing to try to spare them. It was a paradox of thought since the men were destined to be worked to death in salt mines anyway. He ordered the slaves released so that they might use their arms to stay afloat, but the iron neck collars were to remain attached so that all who survived and were found on shore would be known as prisoners. At the last moment, the Roman soldiers and all the passengers leaped into the churning water. As Quartus entered the sea a wave slammed a piece flotsam from the ship against his head rendering him unconscious. Eliab swam to the centurion as the Roman began sinking beneath the waves and held Quartus' head above the water until those who had already made it to the shore were able to throw a rope. Eliab took hold of it and wrapped it around his shoulders while still clinging to the centurion. Those on shore were able to pull both men to safety with great difficulty. Quartus' wound was treated as best anyone could and, after a few hours, he regained his senses.

A soldier asked, "Sir, how does your head feel?"

"Like I had been kicked by a horse! The last thing I remember was jumping from the ship. How did I get to shore?"

"The prisoner named Marcus kept your from drowning."

"Do you mean the Jew, Eliab, saved my life?"

"Yes sir. You would have certainly died if he had not come to your aid."

"Bring the salve to me." Eliab was brought to where the centurion rested with his back against a rock. "Why did you not let be drown when you had the chance?"

"Why would I do that?"

"Because you have already been convicted of killing a soldier during a previous shipwreck."

"What happened then was an accident for which I was falsely accused. I am also a different person than I was before I arrived on Patmos and met the Apostle John. My instinct was to keep your head above water until we could be rescued, and so I did, with God's help."

The hardened officer was skeptical of Eliab's motives. "Perhaps you thought you could make amends by saving me so that you might be set free."

"No sir, I will pay the penalty even though I feel it is unjust. I may have to live the rest of my days in chains, but my spirit is free and my soul is at peace."

The centurion sat up straight and gazed at Eliab. "Jew, if what you say of yourself is true; that you have been wrongly convicted and sentenced to slavery, and if I were in your position, I would be so angry I would want to take my revenge."

Eliab confessed, "I did feel that way when I arrived on Patmos, but meeting the old man named John changed my life. I am a servant of only one person now; he is my Lord Jesus, the Messiah."

"So, you are one of those Christ followers. Well, so be it. At least it is better than being obligated to a Jew."

"Oh, I am still a Jew, but I am now completed in my faith because I have been forgiven by God and have been adopted into his family."

"You make no sense! You must have also been hit in the head. Take him back to the others."

Without a ship to transport the five prisoners who survived the disaster, the Romans marched their captives inland until they found a village. It was there that they commandeered enough horses and a wagon to continue north through Dalmatia to the port of Solona where they waited for another ship that would accommodate the soldiers and their prisoners. After several days the ship arrived and transported them to the north end of the Adriatic where they debarked to begin an arduous journey over land.

Quartus led his men and prisoners toward the great mountains that lay between them and the salt mines. The first part of the trek was through valleys and over high Alpine mountains. Fortunately it was summer and the weather was favorable. Snow remained at the highest elevations but the passes were open. After days of hard climbing and walking, the body of prisoners and soldiers achieved a long valley that snaked northward between nine thousand foot high Alpine peaks. All throughout the Salz River valley, at intervals of approximately twenty miles, the Romans had built small fort-like outpost to guard the trade route.

Along the way two prisoners died of exhaustion, but Eliab did well on the march. He had gained strength working the quarry on Patmos and sharing some of the food delivered to the Apostle John. His ability to keep up with the soldiers impressed Quartus and he slowly began to have a feeling of good will for Eliab. God's man and Rome's man had conversations around the fire at night and the centurion learned of the conversion of Eliab's father, Andrew, and more about how Eliab came to faith in Jesus.

By the time the odd company of soldiers and slaves arrived at the salt mines south of the Roman town of Iuvavum, located on the sweeping eastward curve of the Salz River, an unlikely bond had developed between Eliab and Quartus. Iuvavum was established by the Romans fifteen years before the birth of Jesus and during the reign of Caesar Augustus. Early in the history of the settlement, there was an enclave of Jews which was made up of those who were part of the Diaspora. This created some tension between the Jews and the Romans in the area.

Quartus was posted by his superiors to oversee a group of the slaves who mined salt from the bowels of the earth. Immediately upon arrival at the mines, Eliab and his fellow prisoners were put to work digging out the precious mineral used for preserving meat and flavoring food. It was as valuable as gold to people of the empire and regions beyond the borders of Roman control.

The slaves' labor created huge underground caverns. Eliab was under the direct supervision of Quartus and given responsibility to look after the safety of the slaves. It was not usual for Roman superiors to care anything about the well being of the salt slaves. There was always a supply of useful captives and criminals who could be sent to replace those who did not survive.

Before sunrise the slaves were led by lantern light into the cold caves and it was after darkness covered the land that they were led by lantern light out of the caves to the squalor of their sleeping places. Once a week the pitiful souls were allowed to bath in a nearby lake under the watchful eyes of Roman soldiers. The water was very cold, but a welcome relief.

The first time the slaves were allowed such a luxury, Eliab noticed one of the prisoners who looked familiar. The near darkness in the mines had made recognition of features difficult. Besides that, there was no expectation of meeting anyone whom he had previously known.

"Onan? Is that you?"

Onan raised his head from the water to see who was speaking his name. A great look of surprise swept over his face. "Eliab! I cannot believe it! You must have done something really stupid to end up in this place."

"My friend, how long have you been here?"

"I don't know. It could be six months."

"How were you captured?"

"You remember the men I chose to go with, well we ran into a trap the Romans had set for us. I was wounded and when I recovered the decision was made that I should dig salt for the rest of my life."

"What happened to the others?"

"Dead! All of them. I am serving their sentence and mine. What happened to you?"

Eliab shorten his answer somewhat because there was on a short time for bathing. "I was making my way toward Greece but the ship went down. In the confusion a soldier drowned and I was accused of killing him. A funny thing happened to me on the way to these salt mines. I was first sent to Patmos."

"I have heard that was a place to do hard time. It sure does not seem like it would be a humorous place to be."

"I did not mean that there was anything humorous. I mean that an odd thing happened. I met the man called the Apostle John; one of the first followers of Jesus."

That fact drew curiosity. "Why would he be imprisoned on Patmos?"

"Because he had become a problem for both the Jewish leaders and the Romans. He had so much influence in the Christian movement that it was believed he should be exiled rather than made a martyr. But that is just part of the story. I shared a grotto with him and he helped me come to faith in Jesus as my Messiah: my Savior and Lord."

Onan was greatly surprised. "I would say that such a thing would have been impossible! You were so against the idea that the Nazarene could be the Messiah."

"Not anymore. I have a peace in me that I cannot explain, but I know that all my sins are forgiven and when this worn out body has breathed its last I will see the risen Jesus face to face in God's heaven."

"How I wish I could know that peace and have such a hope."

"You can. Let me explain what I have come to know."

There on the edge of the lake, Eliab led Onan to faith in Christ and the two men rejoiced together. Though their bodies were in Roman bondage they were free from the bondage of sin.

Eliab Marcus and Onan stood out from all the other salt slaves in how they put their backs into the labor as though they felt it was their duty to do the very best they could. When Eliab spoke to those around him, or to the guards, he was civil and circumspect in what he said. Soon, others wanted to know why he bore his burden so well and that gave him opportunities to witness of his faith in Christ and of his hope for a better life beyond this world.

Eliab was often heard quoting something the Apostle Paulus had

said to him in Ephesus: "For me to live is Christ and to die is gain."
Those who had no hope of heaven found the statement to be hollow and
smacked of wishful thinking. How could anyone who had to spend the
rest of his life underground digging salt out of the earth believe in God
and in a life after the last shovel full of the suffocating crystal was dug
and last salty breath was breathed? Eliab always replied that the answer
was found in the Savior who died to pay for sin and who came forth
alive from the tomb to guarantee his follower their own resurrection
from the grave.

One very frosty morning as the slaves made their dreary way below
ground to dig out the "white gold" a man named Archaius, who was from
Macedonia, asked Eliab why he was not grumbling and complaining
like the others. "What makes you so different?"

"The short answer is my faith in Jesus the Messiah. He is my Lord
and loving master."

Archaius laughed. "You call him a loving master? How is it he leaves
you in captivity to these Romans? I have heard the name of Jesus, but I
also heard the Romans killed him."

"The Romans were the instrument used by God the Father to
sacrifice Jesus for the sins of the rest of us."

Archaius scoffed, "I have never heard of such a god. He sacrifices
your Messiah and he allows you to be a slave in the salt mines. Why
would you not be angry at such a god?"

Eliab smiled at the doubter. "The wisest man I have ever heard of
wrote, 'It is better to be a living dog than a dead lion.'"

Archaius grunted his disgust. "And that is supposed to mean
something to me?"

"That isn't all to the saying. It goes on, 'For the living know that
they shall die, but the dead know nothing.' You see, the dead have
left everything behind: both the poor and the rich, the weak and the
powerful."

"Again I ask, what does that mean to me, a slave who is condemned
to be worked to death in these mines?"

Eliab thought for a moment. "Let me put it this way: Would you
rather be a dead Caesar or a living slave?"

Archaius answered, "Are you giving me a riddle? Of course I would rather be anything, including dead, if I could end this misery. It would not matter if I had been a king or a slave."

"Archaius, it does matter. If you are still alive, even though you are someone's slave, there is hope, but if you are dead, there is no hope, even for the Roman Caesar, unless….!"

"Unless what?"

"Unless the one who died for your sins and mine came back to life so that those who put their trust in him will also be victorious over death. In this truth there is hope for both the rich and the poor while they still live. Would you like to have hope of a life beyond the salt mines and beyond the executioner's block?"

"Who would not want to have such hope?"

One of the guards shouted orders to Eliab and Archaius. "You two over there! Stop talking and bend your backs! You are here to dig, unless you would rather feel the lash!"

Eliab thought, "*Satan is at work in this place. He would cheat Archaius out of the gift of eternal life, but I will find another time to share the good news of Christ with him.*"

It was a long time underground before the slaves were permitted to drag their exhausted bodies out of the mine and to a place where they could sleep awhile. It was then that Eliab finished telling Archaius how to receive God's gift through faith in Christ. By the power of God's Spirit another life was changed. Archaius received the unmerited favor of God through Jesus the Savior.

"Archaius, my brother, not even death can rob you of your soul's freedom. I will see you in heaven and we will rejoice for eternity while those who refuse God's love will never know peace. Give praise to God brother! Give praise to God!"

*

Quartus, the centurion, had been strict but fair in his treatment of the slaves. He became harsh only to those who broke all the rules and rebelled against the labor they were required to perform. Even when the lash had to be employed on the back of a hard-headed man, the centurion made it the minimum number of strikes.

Quartus had spent time in Rome when the Apostle named Paulus was confined to prison under close guard while awaiting execution. He heard the Apostle testify that whether he lived of died, Christ was all to him. Eliab had heard those words when he met Paulus in Ephesus and it was not until he was imprisoned with John on Patmos that he came to understand the meaning for himself and he chose those words as the reason for his own continued existence. That statement of faith was eventually completed in Paulus' life when the final appeal of his sentence was heard in Rome and rejected.

The witness of Eliab's life by word and deed, and also the fact that he had saved the centurion from certain death, softened the Roman's heart to the point that Eliab was able to secretly lead Quartus in the sinner's prayer of confession of faith just before the soldier was assigned again to Rome.

"Sir, now that you have come to faith in Christ and are a new man in the eyes of God, would you find another way to make your living rather than being a soldier for Rome?"

"Eliab, I can no more stop being a soldier than you can stop being a prisoner. Our fates are set. A soldier is a soldier until he dies in battle, is severely wounded and can no longer serve, or becomes too aged to fight. Most of us never reach that stage in our lives. No, my brother slave: you are a slave to the salt cave and I to my Roman masters, but we each will find some way to serve our Christ where we are, whether here or in Rome."

*

The overseer who replaced Quartus; a centurion named Tripartus, was a cruel and hate-filled task master who seemed to take pleasure in making an already inhumane situation much worse. He especially did all he could to break Eliab and force him into a retaliatory act that would make his witness seem to be a lie.

If Eliab failed to stand strong in his faith, Tripartus and Satan would win the battle, but Jesus' salt slave would rather die than give an ounce of satisfaction to the enemies of the Master. To compromise, or to falter in his stand for righteousness, would mean that all of Eliab's witnessing and efforts to win the lost souls around him to faith would go for nothing.

The day came when life took a sudden turn for Eliab Marcus. He was in the salt cave working hard as always when a man whom he did not know by name collapsed. Eliab started to attend to the fallen salves when a guard stepped between them. Eliab was shoved aside and the guard struck the fallen slave across his back and ordered him to stand, but the man was unconscious. The guard struck him again and again. It was more than Eliab could tolerate. He grabbed the rod from the guard's hand and when the guard rushed Eliab, his reaction was to raise his arms to ward off blows. In so doing, Eliab inadvertently struck the guard on the side of his head as two other guards grabbed God's man, threw him down, and began to beat him into unconsciousness.

When Jesus' salt slave awakened from his beating he found himself tied to a post above ground and in an atmosphere of cool veiled mist that hung like a curtain. It dampened everything it touched and obscured the giant pine forests that surrounded the mines and the encampment.

Having been without sunlight for such a long time, it was difficult for Eliab to keep his eyes open in spite of the filtering moisture. Realizing that their prisoner was conscious, the guards roughly stood him up and secured his hands more tightly to the post so that he could not sit or stoop.

Tripartus would normally give the task of lashing a slave to one of the guards, but in Eliab's case he chose to do it himself. With great satisfaction he ripped open Eliab's back with repeated swipes of the bone tipped leather straps. Tripartus became weary at the task and stopped to catch his breath. Eliab spoke words that were almost inaudible. "You beat me unjustly. I appeal to Ceasar. It is my right as a Roman citizen."

The anger that motivated the extreme beating suddenly faded as Tripartus looked at the Roman guards who knew that he had gone beyond all reason. He dropped the whip and then turned and walked off in the direction of his quarters. The guards loosed Eliab from the post and carried him to a shed where he was shackled to a wall to await his fate. He languished there with little water and not much food for days before the transfer could be arranged. On the fourth day of his confinement Tripartus had Eliab brought out by two guards. Instead of having him executed on the spot, the Roman officer expressed his great disdain for the battered salt slave as he growled out his command, "Send this one to Rome! Let Emperor Domitian decide what to do with him!"

CHAPTER TEN
Transferred to Rome

Cold breezes and a driving wet snow greeted the prisoners and their guards while only a hint of light filtered through the pines trees that surrounded the alpine mountain encampment near the salt mines. It was time to go back underground for all of the slaves, except Eliab Marcus who was being roughly pushed into a small wagon drawn by two stout horses. With Eliab were three Roman soldiers. The one in charge carried a leather pouch containing orders for the disposition of the prisoner. Eliab was accused of attacking a Roman soldier. This was added to his other serious charges. It was going to be a long and grueling journey from the Alps to the capitol of the Roman Empire.

The trail south through the Salz River valley followed a crude and often jarring path that was beginning to be covered by an increasingly heavy coat of white. The Roman outposts overlooking the trail were often obliterated by the falling snow and could easily be missed. It was essential that the guards and their prisoner find one of those scattered havens before nightfall when the temperatures would plunge to below freezing.

The traveling was exceedingly slow and the soldiers groused over their duty. Guarding the slaves at the salt mines was bad enough, but being responsible for taking Eliab all the way to Rome in the winter was doubly irritating. Oblakan, a recruit from one of the conquered tribes, expressed his feelings. "It would have been better for all of us if Tripartus had just ordered this miserable creature beheaded."

The officer in charge added, "We have our duty! It doesn't matter if we agree with the centurion. As for me, I will be glad to get back to Rome, even if it is only for a few months."

"But, sir, what is so important about this one slave that he should be sent to Rome for trial?"

The guard in charge of the mission answered, "I know it seems odd, but that is for others to understand."

There was no way for these men who know that God was working His will in the matter. These were not ethnic Romans. They had been recruited from conquered people and given the worst duties while true Romans enjoyed the better opportunities that could be found in the empire's army. Rome had been spreading its boarders so far and its army so thin over the vast empire that there were not enough ethnic Romans to fill the ranks. The diversification of nationalities within the forces that were needed to guard the interests of the empire was also diluting its ability to maintain a strong cohesiveness. The issue portended greater problems for the future of Rome.

Eliab was not concerned about Rome's future. He wasn't sure of how long he had to live, let alone allow himself to be distracted by the political uncertainties that existed and were destined to become worse. He reminded himself that his purpose for continuing to exist was Christ Jesus and sharing with others the gift of God's great forgiveness. Eliab thought of the words the Apostle Paulus shared with him while he was still denying he needed a savior.

Years before, when Eliab questioned the Apostle about the truth of Jesus being raised from the dead, Paulus reasoned that if Christ was not raised, then there was no hope for anyone and all people would die in their sin. But Paulus affirmed most vigorously that Jesus was raised and there is life beyond earth. He had personally been with the risen Christ. This truth was Eliab's joy and comfort. He also knew in his own heart that God's Spirit resided in him and would always be with him in life and in death.

Evening was gathering and the gigantic mountains blocked what little sunlight remained. The travelers were between outposts and it was necessary for someone to walk ahead of the horses and wagon with an oil lantern to light the way to safety. Ironically, Eliab was ordered to carry the light and show the way. It was a metaphor of the spiritual purpose of his life. He would not only carry the lantern, he also carried in his heart and in his mind the very light of life, the Lord Jesus, and he would take every opportunity to hold Him high that others might find their way to God.

"Sir, I will be of little use to you if my feet become frozen. Allow me to empty some of these sacks of their contents so that I can wrap the cloth around my feet for more protection."

The request was granted. None of the soldiers wanted to walk through the snow. They were happy to have the slave show the way. Eliab used a pole to stab the ground where it seemed the trail should be as the group made slow progress southward.

Five miles after Eliab was ordered to lead the way through the deepening snow, the party of soldiers and their prisoner came to an outpost situated on a high knoll. Dagar, the Roman officer, gave a shout to warn the fort of their approach. "Hail to those in the fort!"

A voice shouted a reply, "Who hails the fort?!"

"We are Roman soldiers on a mission from the northern salt mines on our way to Rome! We request shelter for the night!"

"Advance and be recognized!"

Dagar went ahead of the others and gained entrance to show his orders, after which the entire group, including horses and wagon, proceeded inside the stockade made up of stones, pine tree logs, and sturdy towers on all four corners. The fortress was not large as such structures go, but was mainly designed to hold a small contingent of troops to protect access into and through the valley. Rome was not the only power interested in the valuable salt. It was a commodity of exchange that could be used by anyone strong enough to take it away from those who labored to dig it from the earth.

A crackling bon fire burned throughout the night in the middle of the enclosure to provide warmth for the soldiers and their animals. Eliab was shackled to a stake close enough to the fire to feel its glowing warmth, but far enough from it that he could not use any of the embers in some way to free himself. Escape was not on his mind. Where would he go if he could get free? He was not prepared for a snowy wilderness and the temperatures that could quickly take the life of someone not clothed properly. If there was to be freedom for him, it would be found in Rome or not at all. He entrusted himself to the will of God.

At first light the guards rousted Eliab and secured him once again upon the wagon with the soldiers. The effort to descend to the valley floor was almost as difficult as it had been to ascend to the fort. The snow had stopped, but it left a deep cover for the trail that made it impossible to detect pits falls and other hazard that might cause a horse to stumble and break a leg. Dagar again ordered Eliab loosed so that he could take a wooden pole and walk ahead of the horses.

By evening everyone was exhausted. Even the horses were tired from making their way through the deep drifts. Another outpost was seen not far ahead. It was there they secured lodging, although it was just as crude as the previous fortress.

On the following morning a weather front pushed up from the south bringing warmer air from the Adriatic Sea. The snow began to melt enough that the trail could be seen without Eliab going ahead of the horses. The good air might not last long and there were mountains to cross before escaping the treachery of the Alps on the way to northeastern Italia and then down the coast.

There were still many days before Eliab would be confined to a prison in the capitol and many dangers once the group left the valley and began picking its way through narrow passes where the wagon might not be able to go. No one wanted to contemplate walking across nine thousand foot mountains, but that might turn out to be the only way to reach the coast.

As the horse-drawn wagon with it four occupants came to the point where the Salz River turned west into the high mountains which were its source, Dagar made the decision to follow the valley west as far as they could, but whenever the terrain began to rise too abruptly they would have to abandon the wagon.

The travelers enjoyed two days of tolerable temperatures and huddled together around fires at night to ward off the drastic change in degrees that came with the loss of the sunlight. Eliab tried unsuccessfully to engage his guards in conversations about their need of a Savior who would forgive their sins and deliver them from a hell that would follow for any who met death without faith in Christ, but he was rebuffed and ordered to keep silent or be beaten.

God's salt slave resorted to the one thing his captors could not prevent: he prayed for their minds to be opened. He prayed also that somehow God would bring about a situation where he might be used to soften the soldier's resistance to what he had to share with them.

The third day of the westward movement brought the group to the six thousand foot level of a mountain range with another two to three thousand feet rising above that. The day also brought a sudden drop in temperature as the flow of air from the south abated and snow began to fall again so heavily that the men could make no further progress. The world for them had become nothing but white so that they could not see the difference between earth and sky.

The soldiers huddle together in the wagon beneath a covering of heavy material. Eliab was left to fend for himself as best he could beneath the wagon. He drew his cloak tightly about him, covered his head with the cloth from a sack, and piled around him what supplies that were left, but nothing he did could prevent his shivering. Snow accumulated thickly and actually became a protection. When the storm slackened and the soldiers emerged from their tent-like covering they found Eliab blanketed with snow. They presumed he had died from the cold, but Eliab moved and shook off the white shroud.

Dagar grumbled, "How is it that you seem to have done better than we?"

The answer came immediately, "God covered me with his mantle."

The men scoffed, but were still in awe that their prisoner had done so well while they were nearly frozen. Dagar ordered a check of the supplies and it was found that the water kegs were nearly empty. He pointed to the other soldiers. "Go to the stream. If there is ice, break it but fill up these kegs or we will only have snow to quench our thirst as we cross over these mountains and into Italia."

Shortly after the soldiers arrived at the edge of the Salz River which had turned into a narrow, iced-over stream, a shout of alarm was heard by Dagar and Eliab. Dagar ran down the slope and found Romula had slipped on the ice and broken through into the water. The other soldier was able to reach his companion before he went completely under and Dagar assisted in bringing the soaked soldier back to the wagon.

Eliab saw the life threatening issue. The soldier's clothes would soon freeze to his skin unless they were removed. "Strip him and put my cloak on him! Get a fire started quickly!"

Dagar bristled with anger. "Who are you to give orders?!"

Never-the-less, he grabbed the cloak that Eliab was holding out to the officer. "Strip him and put this own him! Get a fire started!"

"But sir, there is no dry wood."

"Use part of the wagon! Break the wood into pieces or use your swords to split it for kindling. Be quick about it!"

"Eliab did not seem to be very bothered by having given up his cloak. In fact, he felt pleased that he could do something voluntarily to aid those who had been so adamantly opposed to anything he had to say. Perhaps this was an answer to his prayers.

Soon the fire began to crackle and produce the life saving heat they all needed, especially Romula who had been soaked in the ice cold stream. As he warmed himself by the fire, he realized that the cloak he was wearing was that of the prisoner. He also knew that it was given freely and without coercion. A slight smiled creased his lips as he looked at Eliab. "Sir, please let the slave come closer to the fire." Dagar motioned for Eliab to draw nearer, but said nothing.

By the time the wet clothes were dry and the soldier was able to put on his own uniform and cloak, the day was spent and preparations were made to make a greater fire to last the night. The soldiers chopped limbs from trees and Eliab carried them to the camp to add to the fire. The green wood eventually dried enough in the heat of the flames to begin to burn. A stock pile of wood was accumulated and the soldiers took turns adding it to the flames throughout the bitterly cold night.

Another dawn brought no change in the weather. The wagon was broken into pieces and lashed to the back of the horses. There was no other choice than to walk through the deep snow and lead the animals with their precious cargo up through a pass between mountain peaks as the party turned back to the south. If all went well, they would be through the Alps and down into a warmer climate in two nights and three days.

On the last night in the mountains the soldiers and their prisoner gathered around a blazing fire. Something had changed since they left the salt mines. They were more relaxed with each other. Dagar had no concern that Eliab would try to escape. He had proven his humanity and that in turn made his guards more human. The hardships of the journey and the caring way that Eliab treated his guards changed the soldiers.

Eliab was certainly changed from his days as a youth when he listened to the discussions between his father and grandfather which often became heated. He was very different from the man who sought the blood of Roman soldiers while fighting with the Zealots.

The seed of truth planted by a young woman and her mother back in Israel was watered at Ephesus by a former Pharisee who had become a champion for the crucified and risen Messiah. The seed rooted and grew into a plant on Patmos at the feet the Apostle John. The fruit of the plant developed and ripened in the salt mines with the conversion of the Roman, Quartus, the Greek, Archaius, and the Jew, Onan.

The former hater of all things Roman had sacrificed to save one of his guards and assist the others to endure the hardships of the Alps. Perhaps this last night in the mountains might also be Eliab's last opportunity to persuade these men that there was a hell to escape and a heaven to gain. He tried, but had limited success. With a passion for the salvation of their souls he explained that God's gracious offer of forgiveness and eternal life was for people of all nations.

The guard whose life he helped to save by giving him his cloak wanted to know more and found a moment where he could speak with Eliab when the other two men were taking their turn at sleeping and were not able to hear. Romula came very close to asking God to forgive him of his many sins and make him a new person, but his fear of being ridiculed by his fellow soldiers kept him from making a commitment.

"Romula, I will keep praying for you until you come to Christ or I go to be with Him."

"I wish I had the courage to follow your Jesus, but my family is so deep into the cults of my people they would turn against me if I believed in the Messiah. And then, there are the soldiers with whom I serve. They would have nothing to do with me."

Eliab nodded that he understood the man's feelings but added, "You must realize that you have a choice of fearing man or fearing having to stand before Almighty God unprotected from the punishment than sin brings upon a person. Your only protection is Jesus."

Eliab could see in the light of the flickering flames the sadness etched on the man's face just before he turned and went to wake up the next watch. The freest man huddled in the cold of the mountain was the slave in shackles. He bowed his head and offered a prayer that God would open the eyes of the men so that his guards could become eternally alive in Christ Jesus.

*

The four travelers emerged from the highlands and began a descent through wide passes toward the lower hills of northeast Italia. There was no further need to continue walking. The wood had been consumed and the horses were well rested. The men divided into twos and all of them climbed onto the backs of the sturdy animals. Riding, even at a slow pace, was far better than continuing to stress legs that were already feeling the effects of their long and arduous journey.

The officer, Dagar, riding the lead horse with Oblakan, turned his mount west into the low terrain in the direction of the Adige River that flowed south for several miles and then turned east to the Adriatic Sea. Where the river made its bend east, Dagar ended following the river and headed into the mountain range that separated him and his party from the Gulf of Genova on the west coast. It was the officer's hope that they might find a ship to take them the rest of the way to Rome.

Although the mountains were steep and rugged, they were not like the treacherous Alps and they were not freezing cold. In fact, after what they had endured since leaving the salt mines the trek through northwest Italia to the Liguranian Sea was a pleasant experience. The Roman soldiers were anxious to deliver Eliab and find some time to recuperate. Eliab, on the other hand, was glad for any delay that might occur. He was not in any hurry to face what was ahead of him, but whatever it was he would accept it as God's will.

Before entering the mountains, Dagar ordered a camp be made. They would spend the night beside the Po River and start early the next morning for the coast. All four men were so tired from the exertion of the past several days, that they all slept soundly. Eliab was secured to Romula by leg irons so that there was no danger of him trying to escape.

The morning light was merely a glow in the east when Dagar used his foot to kick each man awake. There was just enough dried meat for each of them to have a small portion and to chase it down with a few swallows of water. Then it was time to get back on the horses and move as quickly as the animals were able to navigate the slopes. By noon the men had achieved a pass through the highlands and began a slow descent toward the water that was still hours away. The first view of the deep blue, glistening waters of the sea lifted the traveler's spirits, including that of the God's salt slave.

At La Spezia, Dagar inquired of the centurion in charge of the port if there was a ship sailing any time soon to Rome. He was informed that it would be four days before one was expected. "It could be sooner or it could be later. There is no way of knowing."

Dagar returned to his companions and their prisoner with the news that they had a choice of waiting for a ship that might or might not arrive in four days, or they could get back on the horses and head south along the rugged coast. Oblakan gave his opinion that if they each had a horse, he would be in favor of continuing toward Rome. Romula indicated that if his opinion counted for anything, he would just a soon wait in La Spezia. He felt they deserved a rest.

The three soldiers turned to look at Eliab, but he made no response. It was not as though they were really interested in his thoughts, but he felt it was curious that they would even hint, by glancing in his direction, that they might, even for a fleeting moment, consider him anything but a piece of meat to be delivered to the butcher shop. That may have been their estimation of Eliab before they began the journey, but there was a slight moderating of their attitude brought on by their shared experiences.

Dagar made the decision. "We will wait for a ship."

There was no choice but to confine Eliab while the others enjoyed their free time drinking and sharing stories with the soldiers stationed at the port. In spite of the good times the guards were having, their thoughts occasionally included Eliab and how he was doing in his jail-like quarters. Romula excused himself from the gathering of his peers and made his way in the early evening to bring Eliab some food and drink. He also wanted to hear more from him about the Lord who forgives sinners and provides them eternal life.

For two hours, Romula listened and asked question about faith, hope, and the love of God. The longer the two talked the stronger the conviction came upon Romula that he needed the Savior. He was convinced that if he were to die that very night, he would go into the pit of hell and its torments. He also was becoming sickened by the picture he saw of himself and the life he had led. With the prison bars between them, Romula begged Elaib's God for forgiveness to wipe away the stain and guilt of his transgressions.

Romula lifted his head from praying and reached through the bars to grasp Eliab's hands. "Thank you for leading me to the Savior. I know things will be hard for me as I try to be true to Jesus, so keep praying for me that I will be faithful. My family gods have had a great hold upon my life. It will be a struggle for me to give them up entirely."

At that moment, Dagar came looking for Romula. "So this is where you have been. It is time to report to our quarters. There is a rumor that a ship might be coming this way tomorrow from the port of Genova. That is not far north of here. We want to be ready in the morning to go on board as soon as it arrives."

Eliab received the news with mixed emotions, but what difference would it make? He would be placed in another prison and it could be weeks or even months before the wheels of Roman justice got around to him. Whether in life or in death, he would share his faith. In Rome, there would be many more prisoners and guards to tell about Jesus. His knowledge of the Scriptures was very limited, but his faith was unshakable. Eliab again quoted in his mind the life principle he learned from the Apostle Paulus. *For me to continue living is Christ and to die is for me, gain.* In spite of his hot and smelly confinement, the salt slave slept well.

CHAPTER ELEVEN
Enemy of the State

The ship from Genova arrived on a cloudless and mildly warm afternoon. Its stay in port was only to let off some passengers and take on cargo. Eliab was considered part of that cargo. He and his guards, who had become companions but not friends, went on board where the salt slave was led below deck and shackled to a supporting beam. Romula was designated to take the first watch of the prisoner, but there was practically no chance that Eliab might be able to escape his bonds.

Oblakan and Dagar enjoyed the beautiful scenery of the calm water and lighter blue sky that met at the western horizon. To the east, there were craggy mountains topped with green that rose abruptly from the water like the blunt end of a loaf of bread that had been torn off by a gigantic hand. Only the swirling and diving birds who grew weary of their almost endless circus-like acts could find space among the openings in the craggy cliffs. The soldiers craned their necks to see the sails above them being deployed to catch what breeze there was to be had.

It was necessary to sail several miles west into the deeper water in order to make the passage between the small island of Elba and the much larger island of Corse. Beyond the Archipelago of Toscano the course was corrected to the southeast where the ship followed the coast of Italia. On the way between the islands, Eliab continued to challenge Romula to forsake all his pagan beliefs and to completely turn his life over to the worship of the one true and living God. Just as Eliab believed progress was being made, Oblakan was sent down into the hold of the ship to relieve Romula.

Attempts to engage Oblakan, who was deeply involved with the superstitions associated with his own cultic gods, elicited no response to Eliab's entreaties. The man spoke a dialect that was a mixture of his European tribe, a version of the dominate language of Italia, and common Greek. Eliab spoke Hebrew, common Greek, and only a colloquial form of the Roman language he had picked up while in the custody of the empire. Even though he could not effectively communicate with the stubborn mercenary soldier, Eliab could pray for the man's soul, which he did audibly in his presence.

It was getting dark and the ship's captain made the decision to move close enough to the coast that he could drop anchor. He wanted to approach the port of Rome the next day in full daylight for reasons of safety. Dagar and Oblakan stayed on deck through the night and Romula slept near where Eliab was secured. As the new day approached, Romula stirred and came over to check Eliab to see if he needed food or water. The humane gesture motivated the prisoner to try again to reach Romula with the message that there was only one God and that he should forsake all other deities. He could not truly be a Christian unless he renounced his superstitions.

"May I share something my father used to read to the family at supper? He often read from the proverbs. I don't remember many of them, but this one has stayed with me. It says, 'Who has ascended into heaven, or who has descended from heaven? Who has gathered the wind in his fist? Who has wrapped up the waters in a garment? Who has established the ends of the earth? What is his name and what is his son's name if you can tell?'"

Romula was quiet for some time and Eliab did not intrude on the man's thinking. When the guard looked back again at the prisoner it was as though he was seeking for something more in the way of explanation from Eliab. "I see you need some help in understanding the proverb. It is this: the one true and living God is the creator. He came to earth in the flesh of a man who is known as the Son of God. It is a title of deity.

The God who created the world and holds it together is the God who, in the form of the Son, made payment for our sins on the cross on a hill near Jerusalem. He loved you and me so much that he was willing to take our punishment."

The soldier listened quietly and then looked around to make sure there was no one who could hear him. "The proverb you have recited confirms for me something I want to share with you, but I am fearful of what may happen if this is made known to others. In the night I prayed again and asked your God to forgive me of my unbelief and to put your Jesus in my life as my Lord and Savior."

Eliab wanted to shout, but refrained from what his heart desired, because there still seemed to be some hesitancy to embrace the Lord Jesus alone as the God of Heaven and as Romula's God, not just Eliab's God. In deference to Romula's fear of others, Eliab prayed softly that the man would find a full and complete release from his pagan beliefs and be a true brother in Christ.

Romula had many questions which Eliab attempted to answer in the remaining time the two men had together before being called up on deck. It was time spent in sharing with the guard words of encouragement and urging him to allow the Spirit of God to lead Romula to others who could give him Christian companionship and make known to him how he ought to conduct himself truthfully when it became known that he sought to become a follower of Christ.

"Romula, there will be times of testing of your faith just as you have seen that I have been tested. Whether the body is at liberty or in chains, you can be a free man in Christ. Be of good courage that when you stand up to the test, you do bring honor to God. Remember that the Lord Jesus has said that whoever confesses him on earth he will confess before the Father who is in heaven."

Eliab became increasingly convinced that what he was enduring because of false accusations and because of his faith in Christ was worth it, in spite of his grim earthly prospects, because others were coming to the Lord. He only wished his grandfather could have found faith in the Messiah.

All hands and passengers were on deck as the ship was eased

into Ostia, Rome's port on the central west coast of Italia. With the gangplank lowered to the dock, the first ones to exist the ship were three Roman soldiers with a manacled prisoner walking between two of them. Transportation arrangements were soon made to take Eliab to his next stop in Rome which was the Mamertine prison located only two thousand feet west of the Coliseum.

The route taken from the port followed the Tiber River to the city of the seven hills. People along the way were used to seeing Roman soldiers and prisoners. It was so familiar that few paid any attention as the wagon bounced its way along the stone surface of the pavement which was a product of slaves and prisoners. The empire was built on the backs of such people.

Rome was on the way to becoming crowded with multiethnic people, so that the native Roman population was becoming diluted and, with that dilution, it became weaker and even more dependant upon other nations to supply its work force as well as to grow the grain that fed Italia. The great city was not so great in many ways. Rome had become a symbol of organized paganism and sexual deviance.

It was for this reason the Apostle Paulus wrote in his treatise to the Romans references concerning the immorality of the grossest kind. He deemed the morally corrupted behavior as being of such an unnatural and animalistic sort that he declared God had given up to Satan for eternal destruction those who practiced such abominations. Rome worshipped everything except the true God.

Emperors found that, to keep the people satisfied and placated and the elite in power, free bread and entertainment had to be provided. Nearly a million souls made there way into the population of Rome and it was described by a writer of the era as a motley cosmopolitan population composed of an influx of foreign rabble. He described the conditions of Rome as filled with annoyances, traffic dangers, fire, and falling houses. The decay was obvious and was also seen in Rome's corrupt politics, immorality, failing infrastructure, obsession over comfort, and its hedonism.

People left the farms for the cities where government subsidies could be obtained. The result of the loss of farming was that Rome had to import much of its grain from North Africa, especially Egypt, as well as the provinces of Mauretania, Numidia, and Cyrenia.

Rome spread its tentacles as far to the east as the Caspian Sea and as far north as Britian, along with Spain, Gaul, and Illyricum, which included the mines where Eliab helped dig the salt the empire needed. On the northern borders of Roman domination were the barbarian tribes of the Vandals, the Ostrogoths, the Huns, and others. Rome could try to absorb these people by conquest or agreements, but the very attempt to keep them in check was spreading the Roman army so thin it only added to the pressure and anxiety of the government.

There was a desperate need for foreign natural resources so vital to the continuation of the empire. Those resources had to be guarded and it became necessary to use conquered people for everything from laborers to teachers to soldiers. This use of foreign people was making the ruling class fat, lazy, and decadent.

The entertainment was the games which began to evolve into blood lust events. There was a great thirst for excitement. What more exciting thing could decadent and idle people want than to see wild animals attack and rip to pieces hapless slaves and other undesirables.

Gladiators dueled to the death or until one capitulated to another; at which time the chief ruler of the games, who sometimes included the emperor, would determine if the conquered fighter should be spared to fight another day or have his head severed from his torso. Such was the barbarism of a people who prided themselves in their laws and ability to govern. Roman society changed from a republic to a dictatorship and soon had sown the seeds of its own demise.

Into the heart of this quagmire of isms and pagan philosophies came a solitary figure. He had no worldly wealth and power. He had no army or navy. He was not a politician nor was he recognized by the elite as having anything to contribute to the Roman view of the world. This solitary man traveled mainly within the borders of his native land and was rejected by his own people for leadership, yet those who became his followers were slowly but surely making Rome take notice.

A force with which no one in the Roman hierarchy of power had reckoned was growing into a universal movement of believers in the deity of an obscure Jewish carpenter who stood up against the abuses of the rulers of his own people. More rapidly than it could have been imagined the followers of this Jesus, whom they believed to be God himself in human form, spread across the empire and took root in city after city. Though initially small in number, they were mounting a passive opposition to the godlessness of the societies in which they found themselves.

This multi-ethnic movement looked upon all people as being equal in the sight of God. It valued all life. It did not tolerate the worship of the pagan deities of Rome, nor would Christians accept the Caesar as a god. This was something the class system of the empire could not stand. No amount of persecution and abuse could stop the flow of ideas from person to person, even in the very confines of Roman dungeons.

It was rumored widely that even members of the royal family had become infected with Christianity. Where the beliefs of these people were not being tolerated above ground, they took to the burial catacombs beneath the city of Rome in order to survive and continue to share their faith in the man whom Rome crucified but who arose from the dead and ascended back to his eternal position of authority, having promised his followers he would return one day to set up his own eternal kingdom.

Another solitary man, a mere mortal named Eliab Marcus, was one of those followers of the Christ. He came to Rome in shackles where the final verdict on his earthly existence would be determined. Who was he? He was a Jew, the grandson of a priest of Judaism. He was a Zealot who fought against Roman authority. He was a prisoner of that great empire, but he was also a liberated soul, having discovered a new life that made him a new person inwardly. Furthermore, this new birth changed his view of the world and the purpose of living in it. He also was powerless as to the things of this world, but in things that were otherworldly he had the words to change men's lives. He had the words of Jesus and they were the power of God unto salvation for all who believed.

The reason for the slave of the salt mines to continue to live, in spite of his many near death experiences, was to capitalize on the opportunities afforded him to show forth the character of his divine Master that others enslaved by the curse of sin could find liberation from both human and satanic tyranny. And if in the pursuit of this new way of thinking and living his physical life should end, then it was indeed gain. Eliab believed that there was nothing better than to be with Christ, whether in life or death.

In a deteriorated area of the great city, at a place dominated by the presence of many Romans coming and going, Eliab was deposited. Some prisoners were shoved about contemptuously as they were transferred from those who brought them to the prison to those who would be their new keepers, but in the case of Eliab there was no such treatment. His delivering guards had made a strange and very unusual bond with him and they reluctantly did their duty and bade him farewell. Romula, was especially hesitant to say goodbye, but Dagar placed his hand on his fellow soldier's shoulder and lead him out into the sunlight as Eliab was taken down two long flights of stone steps deep into the dark dungeon that would be his temporary new home.

Eliab was shoved into a smelly cell contaminated with every kind of corruption. The force of the push sent him reeling to the floor with his back against the cold stone wall. He sat there for a moment to allow his eyes to further adjust to the darkness. A raspy voice out of the darkness indirectly addressed Eliab. "Look gentlemen, we have a guest."

In reply to the voice there were a few grunts and some laughter. Eliab asked, "How many are there of us."

Alpheus responded, "About ten too many."

There being no further indication that the one vocal person had more to say, Eliab began to notice the faint perimeters of his new environment. Indeed, it was crowded. Fortunately, he had not landed on anyone of the other nine occupants of the small dungeon cell. There was some straw on the floor, but mostly stone on which to place one's head. Rustling through the straw were some unidentified small creatures; most likely they were rodents.

"You who spoke to me, what is your name?"

"Are you wanting to invite me to supper?"

"That would be nice if I could, but I assume that dinner is not served in this class of a hotel."

"Oh, a dead man with a sense of humor! I am called Alpheus, because I am the first son of my long departed father."

"I assume you are Greek."

"Assume anything you wish. It is a free country!" There was a smattering of laughter. With his attempt at humor, Alpheus began to cough the cough of a man with very bad lungs.

"How long have you been in this place, Alpheus?"

"Long enough that I am ready to die and get it over with."

"Yet you retain the ability to make a joke of a dire situation."

"Dire, he calls it!" The man began coughing again. Others grunted in a disapproving way.

Eliab believed that men in such conditions would be disapproving of everything, including conversation, and he was about to be swallowed up by silence that only added to the pitiful circumstances.

After several minutes Eliab made a request. "Alpheus, sir, you called me a dead man, but I am very much alive and will remain so."

"Gentlemen, he called me, sir! I don't think that has ever happened before. Well, mister politeness, what is your name?"

"Eliab Marcus."

"You are the one that just arrived by ship. You are the Jesus man!"

Since Eliab considered himself an infant in the faith he wondered how it could be that he was known, especially to a prisoner in Rome. "What do you mean? How do you know anything about me?"

"I have ears. I hear the guards talking among themselves. Dispatches from the north country arrived before you did. Seems like you must have taken the long way to get here. I said you are a dead man, because only dead men end up in this place as fodder for the arena. The Roman's make sport of us and then show us mercy by killing us."

Eliab redirected the subject. "You heard me say that I am alive and will be, even when I am dead. Shall I explain what I mean?"

Alpheus laughed. "Now that is a riddle if I ever heard one. You are alive and you are going to be dead, but will still be alive. Now that is a real trick! I am tired of talking and tired of riddles!" A strong bout of coughing followed the last comment.

Eliab felt the rough wall behind him and realized there were markings etched into the stone. He ran his finger across the scratches and determined that it was the outline of the body of a fish. The marks indicated a fat body with split tail fins. There were other markings he could not distinguish by touch alone. "Does anyone know what the outline of a fish on the stone wall means?"

There was nothing but silence. Unlike the silence that already existed, this was a deliberate attempt to give no answer to Eliab's question. He waited, but the lack of a response continued. "All right, let me tell you what I know. The word for fish in Greek is *ixthus*. Does that mean anything to any of you?"

Alpehus broke the silence. "Are you trying to deceive me? Are you really the Jesus man the soldiers have been talking about, or are you a stooge for the Romans? If you are who you say you are, then you know what the symbol means."

"I can only tell you that I do not know what the symbol stands for, even though I know a word in the Greek language that means fish. I have been in prisons from Asia to an island in the Aegean, to the salt mines near Iuvavum, and now here. I certainly would not cooperate with the Romans against anyone. Though I have asked the one true and living God to forgive me of my sins, I still remember the day my loved ones died when the soldiers attacked Jerusalem and left me an orphan."

Alpehus crawled around cellmates to get next to Eliab. "You said that you asked for forgiveness. How have your received this grace?"

"Yes, I received it as a gift from God through my Messiah Jesus."

"And what did you have to do to be forgiven?"

"I did nothing to earn it. Salvation is a gift of God."

Alpheus pressed his questioning. "And you believe this with all your heart, even though you are a Jew?"

Eliab responded. "Do you find that strange? After all, Jesus was a Jew as were the Apostles."

"Tell me, my friend from the salt caves, have you ever met any of the Apostles?"

"Yes. Paulus in Ephesus and John on Patmos."

"And you did not come across the fish symbol?"

"No, I have not."

The inquisition continued "What was the occupation of some of the Apostles?"

"My father told me than many were fishermen. Oh, now I see the connection."

"Eliab, if I was to meet you outside of prison and wanted to let you know that I am a follower of Christ, I would make the mark of the fish symbol in the dirt and that would let you know I am a Christian. You could respond in the same way and those who are not believers would think nothing of it."

"Do you mean…?"

"Yes, my brother, I too am a Christian. I had to say all the things I did to test you. There are some who call themselves brothers who are false. You should also know that the word for fish in Greek is a confession of our faith. The Greek letters stand for Jesus, Messiah, God, Son and Savior. These are all the things our Lord is to us. If someone cannot tell you this, he or she is to be watched carefully until there is evidence of their salvation."

Eliab felt a surge of euphoria that he had met a true believer. "I, my brother Alpehus, still do not understand how someone like me who has been isolated from the world by prisons, held on board ships, and buried in a salt mine could be known all the way to the capitol of the empire. I am no person of importance."

Alpheus began coughing and then regained his breath. "The Lord does things we cannot understand and He uses people who accomplish his wonders. Do you remember a slave named Archaius?"

"Yes. I was with him in the mines. He confessed Jesus to be his Savior."

"And do you remember a centurion named Quartus?"

"Certainly! He came to faith in Christ only a few days before being transferred from the north to Rome."

Alpheus happily confessed, "I have met them both. They each have kept the faith they learned from you. From few comes many. Christ Jesus takes your little and makes much from it. You think you are weak, and so you are, except when the Spirit of our God makes you strong. You and I will have to be strong for what is ahead of us."

In an extended conversation with Alpheus, Eliab discovered that through a chain of associations between prisoners and jailers, that some of the older prison guards had met the Apostle Paulus years before. A fest of the guards had spent a great deal of time hearing the message of Christ through the Apostle and listening as he dictated letters to the churches he planted in Asia. That exposure to truth led to several soldiers becoming believers. Since Paul and Peter left earth for heaven the underground church needed more strong leadership to guide the believers that were spread throughout Rome's social order. This was on Alpehus' mind as he spoke with Eliab.

"Somehow, you must escape this captivity and be a leader among the scattered believers in this city. People with your faith are sorely needed because of the persecutions our people are facing."

"Alpheus, you cannot be serious. I am not learned beyond what I absorbed as a Jewish child. I am still very new to the doctrines Jesus gave his followers. No, not even if there was a way out of this pig sty, could I be a leader."

"My brother, do not say no to God's call. You have a gift of leadership. It must be used. You also have the gift of evangelism which you have demonstrated to be true. The Holy Spirit and other believers will school you in the doctrines."

Eliab protested, "Why not you? You obviously are more knowledgeable than I."

"I am half dead from weak lungs and too many beatings. I will make my last stand in the arena one day soon. It is there I will triumphantly shout glory to my Savior before the heathen as I breathe my last breath. As for you; there may be a way to do more good before your time comes."

Exhausted from the long journey from the Alps to Rome and from all he and his new friend had discussed, Eliab leaned back against the wall and was soon soundly asleep. Two more nights and days passed with only mutual encouragement being exchanged between brothers in Christ to fill the time. On the fourth night, Alpheus drew next to Eliab and whispered, "It is arranged."

"What is arranged?"

"Your freedom."

Eliab thought Alpheus had lost his senses from his many privations. "There is no way out of this place."

"If you have the right contacts and know the right guards' needs, all things are possible. Or do you not believe our Lord can do all things?"

"Of course I believe, but does God sanctify bribery?"

"Now you are getting too theological. In the morning, the guards will be changing and there is always much confusion. A guard you may know will come for the purpose of taking you to a hearing before a magistrate. He will have orders to present to the keeper of the keys. With God's help, you will walk out together and he will deliver you to a safe house."

"But that will put him in jeopardy. What will become of him?"

"I cannot know that, nor does he. We do what the cause requires of us. Perhaps nothing will happen to him."

Eliab could not sleep that night. At the morning change of guards he was fully awake and anticipating the unfolding of the unknown. His heart raced as he waited for someone to come to the cell door and call his name. Soon, he heard the keeper of the keys call, "Eliab Markus, come to the door! All you others stay where you are!" Next to the keeper was a familiar face. It was Quartus with a paper in his hand. There was every effort to mask recognition. Only their eyes met momentarily. Eliab turned back to look at Alpheus, but he could not see the man's face in the shadows. All he saw was a slight lifting of one hand as a gesture of goodbye.

The heavy door was unlocked and the keeper pulled Eliab out as he quickly slammed the door shut again and turned the key. Quartus hastily placed shackles on Eliab's wrists and ankles. Walking up the flights of stone steps and out through lobby of the prison as if he owned it, Quartus led Eliab back into the bright sunlight and into the grasp of two more soldiers, whom Eliab later discovered were not soldiers, but believers dressed as Roman troops.

The three men with Eliab in the midst of them marched down the stone street, around two corners and then into a doorway where there were two more people who had fresh cloths and sandals for Eliab.

Quartus and the two "soldiers" dispersed while Eliab was taken down another street for several blocks and into a third floor room of a house. It was there that he was able to bath for the first time since he had done so in the icy cold waters of the Alps. Before he undertook any new adventures there had to be plenty of rest and good food to eat.

CHAPTER TWELVE

Grace Triumphs

The underground Church of Jesus the Messiah had suffered greatly with the loss of the Apostles, Paul and Peter. The elderly John had not reached Rome. By the time he was released from Patmos and returned to Ephesus he was near death. All of the original leaders of the Christian movement were at home in Glory with their Master. The Church needed more men of God who were not afraid to die for Christ and the spreading of the message of salvation.

For some reason, it was thought that Eliab could be one of those new leaders, even though he counted himself to be a pitiful excuse for such a responsibility. Yet, if it was God's will, he would lend himself to the task and do whatever the Lord enabled him to accomplish.

The plot that was hatched to secure Eliab's release from prison was successful. The next step was to acquaint him with the labyrinth of the catacombs under the city where many believers who were under great threat found refuge while others continued the work on the surface and among the teeming population. He began immediately to organized trustworthy men to act as shepherds of the flock of God's people. Each shepherd had a certain number of known believers to disciple and to equip them so that they could effectively share their faith in methods and ways that would not draw great attention to them from the opposing Romans who were intent on destroying every Christian they could find.

Eliab began to learn the alleys and narrow gaps between buildings which he used to deftly move about the city and keep in touch with the Church's leaders. From time to time he resorted to the third floor room where he had been taken right after his escape from prison. There he could plan and pray. There he was tutored by older believers in the teachings of Christ and those writings of the Apostles that were being circulated throughout the empire.

The ruse by which Eliab was liberated from his dungeon cell became known and a city wide search began to try to capture him and discover those who were party to the plot. Capture meant sure death by the most horrible methods the Romans could devise. The lady of the safe house cautioned Eliab almost daily to keep his conversations and prayers in a low voice. She said, "These buildings are not constructed like those of the ruling class and their favorites. These walls are thin and one never knows who might be listening on the other side. A great number of Rome's structures were hastily erected and posed a danger to great sections of the city, if one should catch fire. The fire would quickly spread.

Bounties were being paid for any news of where a Christian could be found. Ironically, Christians were being charged with "atheism, treason, and following the ways of the Jews." The efforts of the authorities bordered on paranoia, so fearful were the elite of the spread of a faith that would not recognize the pantheon of Roman gods and goddesses: the Caesar's spirit being one of those gods. The effect was that Christians were looked upon as traitors to the empire and all traitors were deemed worthy of death without trial, although some were afforded the sham of a mock trial.

Eliab moved about the city in the disguise of an elderly beggar dressed in shabby clothes with a clay cup hung about his neck intended for donations which seldom were received. He used a crooked stick to help support his hunched over posture. Charity was not prevalent in the Roman society where the elite and their chosen friends were not disposed to give to the poor and where the poor had nothing to give.

On occasions when the former salt slave, who was now a hunted fugitive, did not need to be disguised he had a calf-length tunic which he carried rolled up and tied with a coarse rope slung over his shoulder. Eliab became quite adapt at quickly transforming himself to whatever his appearance required. It was simply a matter of unrolling the tunic and slipping it over his ragged clothing when he was meeting with a cluster of believers in a home or in the catacombs.

Eliab was able to contact the various "flocks" of believers to discover their needs and to pass on to the new converts what he had himself recently learned from older Christians who had been tutored by people like Paul. What privilege it must have been to have been under the teaching of that great Apostle. Secrecy of meeting places and times was essential.

Only a handful of believers would gather at a place, so that if they were discovered by those who were charged with finding and arresting Christians, they would only capture a few. Times and places of such gatherings were known only to those who were to attend.

The alleys and narrow passageways between buildings were traveled mainly by thieves and other people of ill repute. It was unlikely that Eliab would encounter a soldier or one of the secret agents of the empire in such places. Thieves and robbers left old beggars alone. They had no money and their clothes were not worth taking. In fact, these were the outcasts and criminals; the very kinds of people to whom the message of Christ made the most impact. They were already humbled by their circumstances and sense of unworthiness.

The Gospel message of forgiveness gave such people hope for the present and the future, but there were many people in the city who would be happy to improve their economic condition by informing on Eliab for the growing price on his head. For that reason he had to be both wise and harmless so as not to draw much notice or suspicion.

At one of the meeting places, a lady named Phoebe taught a small group of widowed women in her little home. Eliab made periodic visits to bring food which he gathered from Christians who were better off than others. Phoebe was also a widow in her late forties. She was attractive and Eliab could not help but take notice of her. He tried not to show his admiration as she greeted him at her door. The early morning sunlight brought out the sheen of her long ebony black hair. Her light brown skin color contrasted with the deep darkness of her hair. Her high cheek bones revealed a mixture of ethnicities.

The woman was the daughter of a Jewish mother and a father from middle Egypt where there were descendants of North Africans who had learned of Jesus the Christ a few years after the Lord's death and resurrection. The Christian faith had been propagated by an officer of the Egyptian government who had been won to the Lord through the witness of a believer by the name of Phillip.

As much as Eliab wanted to make frequent visits to speak with Phoebe and just be close to her, he knew that his efforts might draw too much attention to the house and it would place the lady in jeopardy. For the sake of Christ and the ministry, Eliab had to deny the emotion he felt when in her presence and the longing he had for her when he was absent. There was no place in his life for such a luxury. Her safety, as well as the safety of many others, demanded that Eliab focus on the cause of the cross and his calling to be a protector of his brothers and sisters in the faith.

Very late on a Friday, the "elderly beggar" made his way below ground among the passageways that led deep into the tombs to spend the night with a group of new followers who were being shepherded by a person Eliab had not met in the catacombs before. He was assured that this leader of a flock knew him, but Eliab could not imagine who that could be.

Arriving at the gathering place he walked up behind the man leading the group in a study of the Apostle John's letters. As the man turned to see who was approaching, there was a joyous moment of recognition on the part of both men. Quartus, the centurion from the salt mines whom Eliab led to faith in Christ and who was instrumental in getting him out of prison, was standing there in common clothing. The two embraced heartily.

"Quartus, you are out of uniform!"

"Old friend, I am no longer a soldier of the empire. Remember that I told you a soldier is one until he dies in battle, is wounded too severely to fight, or is too old to serve. Well, there is one more reason to no longer be a soldier: I am a soldier of our Lord. I no longer carry a sword and shield to destroy other men. However, Eliab, I carry the sword of God's message that cuts deep into the heart of a sinner to bring that person to an understanding of how, through the Lord, there is escape and freedom from the curse. And I carry the shield of faith to defend against spiritual wickedness in high places as well as to smother the fiery missiles of the evil one who seeks to reclaim me."

"Quartus, my brother, Satan may test you and cause others to harass you, but you have been bought with the price of the blood of our Savior and you belong only to God in life and in death."

"Yes! And I rejoice in that knowledge."

Eliab was curious and asked, "When did you begin to meet here in this place and with these believers?"

"Only recently. I came to a decision and was able to make contact with someone I suspected of being a follower of our Lord. I took the risk of revealing my faith. Soon thereafter I was led at night into the catacombs and I have been in this area for the last two weeks. I was able to obtain food that I brought with me for these people. I have reason to believe that I am being hunted."

"I too, my friend. I have been using a disguise to move about the city. I believe it is not wrong to deceive the devils who would destroy the Church."

Quartus admitted, "I knew when I took off my uniform I would be considered a traitor to Rome."

"Then why did you do it?"

"Because I could no longer obey many of the orders given to me or make those who served in my command obey them. The orders were against the things Christ taught and I could not do them."

"Such as?"

"Such as taking people like you to the dungeon beneath the Coliseum to be used as sport by the gladiators, or staked out in the arena for wild animals to devour for the entertainment of the masses."

Eliab grasped his friend's hand tightly. "How I admire your decision and your courage. I also admire your Christ-like spirit. You are needed down here to care for the sick, the fearful, and the homeless who have escaped the grasp of the enemy with their lives and nothing more. Are you able to defend your fellow Christians if it comes to that?"

"I have wrestled with that thought. Until now the catacombs have provided a refuge; a sanctuary, but that may not last. Emperor Domitian is determined to root out every believer. Someday the dedicated antichrist forces will venture into these burial chambers and then I must decide whether I will be able to use my skills as a soldier on behalf of these people or die with them.

"Quartus, you are a trained leader and the Church here in Rome needs a man of your abilities. I urge you to do all you can to safeguard these beloved souls."

"I understand that you have done much, Eliab, to help spread the message of our Savior."

Eliab revealed his inner most feelings. "I believe that my days for doing this work may be few and I want to know that the ministry is in the best hands."

The two men sat and talked for hours. In that time they learned a great deal more about each other than they had ever known. Quartus discovered that his former salt slave was the grandson of a priest and the son of a wealthy businessman. Eliab learned that Quartus was of the noble strata of Roman society. His father was a senator and, because of that position, the son gained his rank of centurion, having also distinguished himself in battles against the barbarian tribes of Britain.

"Well, most excellent Quartus, we are not political even though political position has been in our back grounds. Our nobility is not from man, but from our God who has made us to be kings and priests and joint heirs with our Savior."

Quartus protested the manner in which Eliab addressed him. "My good friend and brother, I do not answer to 'most excellent.' I am a servant of the Most High God, as are you. We may not die the death of nobles, but we will surely rise to glories this world will never know until Christ returns and is Lord over all."

Dawn crept across the ancient city and peaked between buildings to send streaks of light down nearly empty streets. Very soon those same streets would be filled with a cross-section of humanity; each person in a hurry to go somewhere, but utterly lost in sin and destined to pay its penalty, unless the Light whom God sent into the world illuminates the spiritual darkness that is their shackles and damnation.

Up from the bowels of the city came Eliab to do his errands of mercy and share the one and only way for a human being to rise from the pit of despair that shrouds the human condition. Only Christ makes alive those who are nothing more than walking dead men. As Eliab emerged from an entrance to the underworld of Rome, strong arms seized him.

"So you thought your could escape Roman justice, did you?" Eliab made no effort to resist. He had a sense that his time as a free man had come to its end and he was ready to make his witness for Christ in whatever opportunity lay before him in captivity. "It seems you have a Brutus in your midst. He has been paid well for his information. If it brings you any satisfaction, Rome does not value traitors of any kind. He will enjoy his new found wealth for only a little while and then he will join you in the prison." The soldiers laughed at the irony that both the informer and the victim would meet the same fate.

Two months of isolation in the worst conditions passed slowly. Eliab had no contacts. There was no one except the door keeper to speak with twice a day. The man did little more than grunt inaudible words as he shoved some soured soup through a slot in the cell door and, later in the day, with the help of a guard, retrieved the waste bucket.

The morning finally came when Eliab was escorted by four guards to the chamber where he stood before a magistrate to receive judgment. He was afforded the opportunity to make his defense before the inevitable sentence was pronounced. There were others in his situation who never received a formal judgment, but were merely transferred to the Coliseum dungeons. Eliab's charges were read. They were enumerated at length which included insurrection, treason, corrupting the loyalty of soldiers, proselytizing, and creating a public nuisance. At the end of the list was the charge of murdering a Roman soldier.

The presiding officer asked for the prisoner to respond and so Eliab did. "Your Majesty, to the charge of murder I plead innocence. To the other charges, I can only say that, whereas I was once a reluctant slave of the empire unjustly sentenced to digging salt from its mines, I have become a willing slave of the Messiah Jesus, spreading the salt of the Gospel to the world in the power of God's Spirit who lives within me. Though my body is in chains, my soul and mind are free."

The magistrate loudly interrupted Eliab. "I have called for you to state your guilt or innocence to these charge; not to give a speech!"

Knowing that this could his last opportunity to give his testimony in a court before witnesses, Eliab continued. "When my journey in this world is over I will be in Paradise with my Lord. Let the empire destroy my flesh if it will, it shall become a mere tool in aiding me to glorify my Savior while I am yet able to declare his name."

"Silence! You are to say no more!"

"God has given me understanding, whereas I was once blind like those who led my people into their own false understanding of God's law. I wish that all mankind could see what is real and what is true, through faith in Messiah Jesus."

"Guilty of all charges!" The court officer motioned to a guard who struck a blow to the back of Eliab's head that dropped him to the floor. He then was dragged unconscious from the place of judgment back to his cell and thrown face down into the filth of that place.

Several hours later the door opened and another body was deposited in the cell. "Here is a companion for you! You might want to execute him yourself. He is the one who informed the searchers where to find you."

The informer withdrew to the far corner of the eight feet by eight feet cell. There was fear in his eyes as he looked at the unconscious Eliab. Since the pitiful creature who had betrayed a man who had been nothing but kind to him, Oblikan feared reprisal and wondered if he ought to strangle the Christian before he regained his senses and discovered who was with him. He crept over close to Eliab just to make sure he was not already dead.

Oblikan hesitated about placing his hands on the former salt slave just long enough that Eliab stirred and rolled half way over onto his side which left him facing Oblikan who lost his nerve and drew back. Eliab's vision was blurred from the clubbing he had received and was not able to focus on the face of his cellmate. "Who are you and how long have I been here?"

"I do not know. I was put here after you were."

Eliab questioned, "Do I know you? Your voice has a familiar sound to it."

There was no reason to try to deny what would soon be obvious. "You remember me all right. I was with you from the Alps to Rome by way of horse and ship?"

"Yes. Yes, of course, you are Oblikan. So, your fate and mine intersect again. But why? I am condemned as an enemy of Rome, but you are a soldier."

The informer became fearful and he looked for anything on the floor of the cell to use as a weapon. "Just stay away from me! Keep your distance!"

"Oblikan, what has you so upset? You know you have no reason to be afraid of me. I am not a warrior."

"Then forgive me for what I have done! I beg you to not hold my transgression against me!"

"So, it was you who told the authorities how to find me. Why have you done this and how did you know where I would be?"

"Oh, please, Eliab, I was desperate! One day I saw through your disguise and followed you. For months I said nothing. At first, all I wanted to do was speak with you, even though it was my duty to help arrest you. When the reward price placed upon you grew so large the temptation was too great to resist. I am so sorry for the awful thing I have done! My superiors blamed me for not revealing your comings and goings long before I did."

"And what of your reward?"

"This is my reward! I am to die with you."

"Would you rather live with me than die with me?"

"Who would not want to live? But there is no escape from here?"

"When I was in Ephesus many years ago, having broken my leg in an accident, I met a man who tried to tell me about the love of God to be found in Jesus the Christ and I would not listen. I told him I had nothing but heartache in my life and great disappointments. I did not see how this

Jesus could do anything for me. I was without family, without a home, without friends, and unable to walk. I felt like everyone had abandoned me, but this man named Paulus, told me that if I repented of my sins and confessed Christ to be my Messiah and Savior, he would be with me at all times and in all circumstances. Paulus said that for a believer in Christ there would be no test or trail in life that would come that was not also common to all people, but that God would hold me close and make a way of escape that I should bear up under the burden."

Oblikan enquired, "And did you believe?"

"No, not then. It was later, as a prisoner on the island of Patmos, I met another man who was a follower of Christ and through his witness the Spirit of God convicted me and won me to Jesus. I experienced forgiveness of my sins. For that reason I forgive you of what you have done to me, but you need a greater forgiveness that only God can give."

"You tried to win me to the faith in the past when I was a free man. I am now condemned to die and what sort of a man would I be if I confessed Christ now just because I fear what is beyond the grave?"

Eliab felt a great compassion for his betrayer. "I cannot help you escape this prison, but God can provide your soul escape from the fires of an eternal hell. Oblikan, if you sincerely asked God to forgive you and save you, and believe it when I say that God loves you and wants you to be in His eternal family, you will be saved and will join me in Paradise."

The man struggled with the decision he had to make. "It is so hard for me to believe that you and God will forgive me."

Eliab answered, "I assure you that it is not being a coward to make your peace with God while there is yet time, but it would be the mark of a fool to refuse to believe in Christ. Will you now call upon the name of the Lord to save you and prepare you for what lies ahead?"

"I will! I do believe! Oh, Mighty God, cleanse me of my many sins and come into my life. I accept Jesus as my Savior! Thank you God for forgiving me!"

Eliab clasped hands with the new convert and prayed for courage for his new brother in Christ. For the rest of the day and into the night the two men rejoiced as Eliab instructed Oblikan concerning God's love and grace. He spoke to him of heaven and the glories that awaited them: those glories he learned from the mouth of the Apostle John.

Two weeks passed before Eliab and Oblikan were transferred to the dungeon beneath the Coliseum. They were placed in a large room that resembled a cattle stall more than it did a dungeon, but it was just as secure. There they spent a week. From time to time, people were herded out in chains and up to the arena. Those poor souls never came back. The crowd noise continuously filtered down to the dungeon on the days the games were in progress. Sometimes the noise became very loud and then would subside. Screams could be heard, but they did not come from the spectators. Everyone knew what that meant.

The hour arrived when Eliab learned that he would be taken to the arena the following day. There was a certain delight the guards enjoyed in trying to ramp up fear in those who were to die by the claws and jaws of the wild animals. Hearing of his date with death, Eliab made a request of the centurion overseeing the guards. "Sir, I being a Roman citizen make a request that I be crucified in the arena."

"You must not know about the prolonged agony of such a death. You would be better off to be killed by the beasts."

"Nevertheless, I ask you to pass on my request. I wish to die by crucifixion."

Hours later the centurion returned with the news that Eliab would be granted his wish. In fact, the master of the games thought it would be a wonderful thing for the people to see. Oblikan said that he would like to join Eliab it that form of execution. The Romans did not know that Eliab chose crucifixion as a way of witnessing of his faith in Christ and he would do his best to shout out to the crowd his praises to the Lord until there was no breath left in him.

The guard added to his report, "You will have company. There will be others of your sect, both men and women, who will meet the same fate. I still believe you are a fool."

"Sir, heaven will reveal who are the fools."

The centurion looked puzzled at the comment and then muttered something under his breath as he turned and walked away.

*

It was a brilliantly sunny afternoon in the month of August when a group of eleven people were led out of the darkness of the dungeons into the Coliseum arena. They tried to shield their eyes, but the effort was prevented by the heavy chains around their arms. These chains were then attached to a metal belt around each person's waist.

The several thousands of people filling the tiered levels of seats overlooking the floor of the Coliseum roared with glee. There was great applause as the prisoners were each made to stand in front of a tall wooden stake. One by one they were pushed to the ground and made to lie down on their faces while a wooden beam was laid upon their backs. Leather thongs that had been soaked in water were used to lash wrists to the beam. When the guards were finished with their work there was still one empty cross.

A team of guards hoisted each of the condemned to a height of eight feet where the cross beam was fixed against the vertical pole. When all eleven were suspended by their wrists, their feet were also lashed by the wet leather to the posts. The position was extremely painful as the body sagged from its own weight and pulled downward, placing great stress on the wrists. There was nothing against which the condemned could push with their feet to try to relieve the downward pressure.

The bodies began to sag even more from the heat of the sun. No water was provided to quench the thirst. Eliab turned his head to the right and saw Oblikan next to him. "God will help you endure hardness as a good soldier of Jesus Christ." A slight smile creased Oblikan's lips as he acknowledged Eliab. Beyond Oblikan there was Onan. Next to him was the lady who harbored Eliab in the safe house. When Eliab looked to his left he saw Romula and Alpheus and others.

A centurion barked a question to the guards. "I thought we had twelve condemned! Where is the missing prisoner?"

"Sir, he was too weak. He died on the steps coming up from the cells."

"Go find me another! Make sure that one is stronger! We want a good show for the people."

A finely robed man in the royal box stood to his feet and crossed his arms over he rather rotund belly and addressed the eleven hanging on the crosses. "Renounce this Jesus of yours! Renounce him as god and pledge your loyalty to Caesar as your god and master and you will be brought down from your crosses and shall be set free!" The self-important man waited for answers.

After a momentary pause, where the only voices to be heard were the muffled speculations of the crowd, Eliab raised his voice. "Sirs, our God and Savior, Jesus the Christ, would not come down from his cross to save himself six decades ago. He would not save himself, so that by his death for your sins and ours all who would believe in him would find forgiveness and everlasting life. We forgive you for what you do to us today!"

The crowd gave a simultaneous gasp at the audacity of Eliab, but he continued: "Sirs, if you will confess with your mouths that Jesus Christ is Lord and believe in your hearts that he is risen from the dead and is seated with the Father in Heaven as supreme judge of all mankind, you will be saved from the everlasting hell that sin deserves!"

The official retorted, "And who are you to declare such notions? You are a criminal about to die for yours sins against the empire!"

Eliab ignored the question that sounded more like an accusation. "I declare to you that God loves you, however the wages of sin is eternal condemnation, but the gift God offers you everlasting life through Jesus the Christ to whom we belong and for whom we willing die to bring glory to his name!"

The man standing in the chief spectators' box again shouted, "Enough of this foolishness! Renounce your false god and you shall live! I swear it!"

Eliab struggled for more air in his lungs as he replied, "We have no God but the one true and living God whose Son we worship. To him be all honor and praise!"

A louder gasp erupted from the multitude of spectators who had gathered to see torture and death, but what they were getting were words their ears did not want to hear."

In the days of Eliab's childhood his father, Andrew, required him to memorize passages from the scrolls of the Psalms and the Prophets. He had not recited any of those since he became an adult, but as pain warred with his spirit to fill the mind and dull the senses, he recalled a passage from the prophets and he began reciting it with as much volume as could be squeezed from his compressing lungs.

Although the words were for Israel in a time of that nation's great iniquity, the prophet's message fit the circumstances of Rome's own degradation. While gasping for breath to speak, Elaib recited, "Oh that my head were waters… and my eyes…a fountain of tears… that I might weep day and night…for the slain…of the daughter of my people. Oh that I had in the desert…a traveler's lodging place…that I might leave my people…and go away from them…for they are all adulterers…a company of treacherous men. They bend their tongue…like a bow…; falsehood and not truth…has grown strong in the land…for they proceed…from evil to evil…and they do not…know me… declares the Lord."

Eliab paused as though memory had failed him. The man in the box ridiculed his effort. "The prisoner is delusional! Take no heed to his ramblings!"

God's salt slave remembered more of the passage. "Shall I not… punish them…for these things?…And shall I not…avenge myself says the Lord?…And shall I not…avenge myself…on a nation…such as this?"

Great moaning cascaded from the people massed in the seats who were anxious for the prisoners to begin to cry out for mercy. There were no cries. There was only silence as the Christians endured their agony and kept it within themselves.

Eliab had raised his warning to the Romans as he felt motivated and empowered by God's Spirit. It was a warning to the leaders of the empire to get ready for God's judgment because of the nation's corruption and Rome's persecution of Christians. And so it will be for any nation that rejects God's grace and does evil against His people, whether Jew or Christian; for God has not abandoned either.

Another scene was taking place that nearly went unnoticed as the people were fixated on the eleven whose life force was ebbing. Some were already near death from having been severely beaten before being brought out to be crucified.

To the left of the crosses stood the centurion in charge who had ordered that another prisoner be brought up from the dungeon to be placed on the empty cross. The centurion began slowly to sink to his knees as he bowed his head. That drew the attention away from all the others.

The man, whose name was Argubus, had removed his helmet and it lay beside him on the ground. Deliberately he stood and pulled his short sword from its scabbard and dropped it beside his helmet. He then unbuckled his breastplate and it fell to the dust at his feet. He looked at the arena master's box and then at Eliab and their eyes met. There was no need for words to be exchanged. It was clear what was happening. God's Spirit was at work.

Argubus turned to the box containing the royal visitors who were all standing in amazement at what they were watching. The centurion spoke slowly but very clearly. "For some gods men will dare to live and do battle. For this God of whom I have just now heard and the devotion I witness from these people who willingly worship him as they lose their lives; to him I surrender myself and I shall serve him who has forgiven me of my sins and unbelief. I choose his love and mercy and I choose to die with these who have more faith and courage than I have ever witnessed in war."

The newest convert on that hot afternoon walked to the empty cross and said to the guards, "This is my last order. Place me on this stake and this beam just as you did the others. Spare me no comfort." And so, Argubus was hoisted to join the other Christians.

In a loud cry of outrage the royal representative of the Caesar shouted, "Traitor! Traitor! You shall not have the glory you seek! Take your spear and end his life! Do it, or you will meet his fate!"

Reluctantly a guard approached his centurion. "Sir, I don't want to do this."

"Allow me to guide your spear." Argubus positioned the point of the spear against his body in the optimum place.

"But sir...."

"Soldier, do your duty!" with an upward thrust into Argubus' body just below the left ribs he was set free from this world.

"End this now! Break all their legs and let these traitors remain on the crosses for the scavenger birds to feast on their flesh!" With that command, the royal box quickly became empty and those in the tiers of seats exited the Coliseum feeling they had been cheated of their sport.

All through he afternoon and into the early evening hours the Christians endure their suffering as a witness to their faith in Christ. The physically weakest of the Christians died first. Others succumbed as the sun became lower in the sky. The last to die was Eliab. His spirit departed right at sunset and darkness engulfed the Coliseum. The guards left the arena by lantern light and took up their posts at the main entrance. Why they were left to guard dead bodies, they could not understand. All they talked about through the night was the action of their centurion.

*

There was only a faint glow on the eastern horizon when other guards arrived the next day to relieve those who had stayed the night. It was their duty to bring slaves out of their cells to remove what remained of the bodies on the crosses. Long, deep shadows still bathed the floor of the Coliseum in darkness as the guards entered to see what they had to contend with and how many slaves would be needed to do the morbid job.

The sun broke its first rays of light broke through the open arches lining the upper stories of the gigantic structure. Sunlight pierced the darkness and flooded the crosses. They were empty!

Confusion gripped the guards as they ran forward and stood in front of the beams of wood that contained not a single corps. One shouted, "What has happened here? Has there been a resurrection?"

Another answered, "Fool, how can there be a resurrection if there has been no burial?"

"Then you explain this and what we must tell our superiors!"

"We tell them what will satisfy them. We don't know what happened, but we can provide an answer they might accept. I fear the Christian God more than I fear our own leaders."

*